The Replacement Bride

CYNTHIA WOOLF

ISBN:
ISBN-13: 978-1-938887-74-1

Photo credits – Romcon Custom Covers and Period Images

DEDICATION

For Jim.

My love, my heart, my best friend and my husband.
Without your support and love, my dreams would
never have come true.

I love you.

ACKNOWLEDGMENTS

Many thanks to my editor Linda Carroll-Bradd, without whom I couldn't write this or any other book. Linda makes me work to bring out the best in my books.

Thanks also to my Just Write partners, Michele Callahan, Karen Docter and Cate Rowan. They always help me brainstorm and bring the story together.

Thanks to Romcon Custom Covers for my cover artwork.

Special thanks to Michele Callahan for writing my blurb for me. They are always wonderful. Thank you, my friend.

CHAPTER 1

March 15, 1873

Jesse Donovan read the letter from his fiancée Rebecca Jane Flynn twice and still didn't believe it. Finally he read it out loud.

March 6, 1873

Dear Jesse,
I know we were planning on being married when I came out to Hope's Crossing in a few weeks. But, I can't. I simply cannot give up living in New York City for some tiny town in the middle of nowhere in the Montana Territory. Do stores exist there or do you have to grow your own food? Can you actually see me

scratching around in the dirt trying to plant seeds?

I've decided to stay in New York and marry Simon Coleridge. He may not have as much money as you now do, but he can keep me in the style I want to be kept. I hope you'll find some nice woman who won't mind living in a little town and getting her hands dirty.

Perhaps you can get a mail-order bride. Several agencies here in New York provide that service. The best known one is Matchmaker & Co. I've included a clipping from the newspaper with their advertisement.

Good luck, and have a happy life.
Rebecca Jane

Jesse crumpled the paper in his hand and threw it across the room. Then he slumped down into his chair and covered his face with his hands. Anger pushed through. He stood up and kicked the chair. Love isn't real. Didn't Rebecca Jane just prove that? He loved her and she dumped him like so much trash. That would never happen again.

He looked down at the clipping that had fallen onto the table when he opened the letter. He still needed a wife and a hostess. A mail-order bride? Him? He wouldn't have to worry about love and Sam Longworth, the sheriff, had done all right. Jo was a beautiful woman who could cook, clean and hunt with Sam, both people and animals. Jo was a bounty hunter before she married Sam but she didn't tell him until she had to when one of her bounties escaped and came after her.

Seems, if he remembered correctly, Sam had used this same mail-order bride company but not the one out of New York. Guess he better go talk to Sam...or Jo. She might be the one to ask about the brides that these places have.

With a shake of his head, Jesse picked up and read the advertisement.

Are you lonely? Looking for a wife to help you and care for you. Someone to have your children and keep your home. Apply at Matchmaker & Co. 221 Baker Avenue, New York City, New York or 467 10th Street, Golden, Colorado. Send your inquiries to the attention of Mrs. Maggie Black.

The office in Golden was closer, so Jesse would write to that one...after he talked to Jo.

He walked down to Sam and Jo's house,

next to the jail. Jesse heard a commotion on the other side of the door and wondered if he should knock but he did anyway.

Moments later the door opened and Jo Longworth stood there with a crying baby in her arms.

"Oh, Jesse. Just the person I need."

She thrust the crying baby at him then hurried into the kitchen.

Jesse jostled the infant to quiet his crying. "Shh, now you're fine."

The baby stared wide-eyed at him.

Jesse followed Jo to the kitchen. "Hello, Paul." Jesse crooned to the baby. "What's the matter? Is your mama being mean to you? Hmm?"

"No," came the reply from the kitchen. "I'm not being mean to him. He needs changing, and I have to get the clothes off the line before he can have a clean diaper. Hold him for a bit, will you?"

"Sure. Holding him reminds me of caring for my baby sisters and brothers."

Jesse sat at the table and held little Paul with his hands cupped around the baby's head and the child's feet at Jesse's elbows, His body cradled and protected from the hard wood by Jesse's arms.

Jo came back inside with a basket full of clean dry clothes. Her pretty blond hair in a bun at her nape, but wisps of hair escaped framing her face in long curls. She was tall and had pretty blue eyes. If he found someone as pretty as Jo, he'd be a lucky man.

"I'll take him now. As soon as I change him you can have him back. He does seem to love you so."

She pulled two diapers off the top, and laid a towel on the table. Then she came over to Jesse and Paul, picking up the baby and changing his diaper on the towel.

"I have a way with babies and small children." But not with women.

"Indeed you do. But you didn't come all this way to take care of Paul for me. What can I do for you? Would you like a cup of coffee?" She jutted her chin toward the stove.

Jo gave Paul back to Jesse and then tackled the folding of the clothes in the basket.

"Yes, coffee would be good."

With the baby in his arms he angled his head and looked at Jo.

"Why did you become a mail-order

bride? You're a beautiful woman. You could have your choice of men."

"I take it you think I'm not good enough," said Sam as he entered from the living room.

"No, it's not that." He didn't want to tell them but he decided he should. "You might as well know. Rebecca Jane has decided to marry someone else and stay in New York City. She didn't want to come to the wilds of Montana and Hope's Crossing."

Jo came over and hugged him around the shoulders, while he sat holding her son. "You deserve better than some rich hoity-toity woman, but I'm so sorry anyway."

Jesse shrugged. "Don't be. I'll just get a replacement."

Sam, tall, with brown hair and mustache, raised his eyebrows. "A replacement...bride?"

"That's right. I'm sending for a mail-order bride. Like Jo."

"Like...Jo?" repeated Sam, glancing toward his wife.

"Yes." Jesse noticed a disbelieving tone to Sam's voice. "Is there something wrong?"

"You do realize how lucky I was to get Jo?" asked Sam.

"He can be just as lucky," said Jo as she went back to folding her laundry. "Are you using the same company? Matchmaker & Co? Mrs. Black is very good and she'll make sure you are who and what you say you are before she sends one of her ladies."

Sam grinned. "She's not as cautious with the girls."

"Not true." Jo shook her head. "She knew I was a bounty hunter, knew everything there was to know about me and accepted me anyway. She said I was exactly what you needed."

"Sounds to me," Jesse put the baby up on his shoulder and stood, "like this Mrs. Black knows more than what we tell her."

"She sends a man to screen you before she accepts you as a client," said Jo.

"I guess I better write her then." He handed little Paul back to his mother. "If I expect to get married any time soon." Regardless of what I think of her process, it's a necessary evil and she does get good results. He looked over at Sam and Jo. Sam was holding Paul now while Jo finished with the laundry. If only I could get as lucky, I'll be a happy man. Won't I? And what about Harry Smith? Is it fair to bring a wife here when Harry's threatening to get even with me for firing him?

March 16, 1873
Dear Mrs. Black,

My name is Jesse Donovan. I'm six feet tall with brown hair, brown eyes and all my teeth. I've included a recent photograph. I am a miner who struck the big one and am now quite wealthy. I am in need of a wife who can serve as my hostess and give me children. My former fiancée decided to remain in New York and marry someone else, rather than venture to Hope's Crossing. I'm looking for someone who will not be put off by living in a small town. I've built a new house, the nicest in town, and need someone to help me care for my home and fill it with children.

I've been referred to you by Jo Shafter, now Longworth. She said that you have the extraordinary ability to pick the right woman for each man, or perhaps I should say the perfect man for each of your ladies.

Yours Sincerely,
Jesse Donovan

April 1, 1873

Home for lunch, Jesse had just finished when a knock sounded on the front door of his home. He went to answer it.

"Mr. Donovan?"

"Yes, I'm Jesse Donovan."

The man at the door was dressed in a nice three piece suit and traveling coat. He was shorter than Jesse which made him average height and had graying brown hair covered with a bowler hat.

"I'm Ernest Lang. I work for Mrs. Maggie Black at Matchmaker & Co. I'd like to talk to you." He handed Jesse a business card.

Jesse stepped back. "Please come in. Would you like a cup of coffee? You can hang your coat on the coat tree there." He pointed to a small alcove behind the door.

Mr. Lang entered and hung his coat. He kept the briefcase he carried with him. "Yes, please. Coffee will be helpful. We might want to do this in the kitchen."

Jesse led the way to his kitchen and wondered what the man would think of his home. The kitchen was the most modern in town. All the countertops were butcher block and the icebox the largest and nicest available with separate doors for the ice box and the food. The stove had six burners with ceramic doors on the oven, the warming shelf and the door to the fire. Jesse got a cup out of one of the oak cabinets and gave the man a cup of hot coffee from the pot on the stove.

He noticed that Mr. Lang was looking all around the kitchen.

"Now," Mr. Lang took a large notebook from the case that he carried. "Mr. Donovan. Please tell me a bit about your background."

"Well, I'm the oldest of eight children. My parents were farmers in Missouri and we were always dirt poor. My father died four years ago. I left so I wouldn't be another mouth to feed and went to New York. There I did well in the stock market doubling and redoubling my money until I had quite the stake, but I wanted more than just enough money for me to live comfortably. I wanted enough money that my mother and siblings could also not want for anything. With this money from the gold mine, my brothers and sisters can go to college and make better marriages. My mother will never have to work again or marry a man she doesn't love just to have a roof over her head."

Mr. Lang made extensive notes in his book. "You said you struck a vein. Was it just you or do you have partners?"

"Just me." Jesse thought about the hard work he'd put in to get the mine to where it is now. A partner would have made it easier, but then he'd have to share the wealth, too.

"What do you see happening in your future?"

"Did you read my letter to Mrs. Black?"

"Yes, I did. I should explain that I want to know what else you want to happen in your future."

"I am working toward Montana statehood and when that happens, I might decide to run for office. I need a woman who can help me to achieve my goals, political or otherwise. But mostly, I want a helpmate and a woman I can count on. A woman who always keeps her word."

"And these are the reasons you're looking for a mail-order bride? Do you have a reason you think women don't keep their word?"

"Yes." He took a sip of coffee to wet his dry mouth. "I'll be honest with you. I'm looking for a bride because the woman I asked to marry me before I came out here decided she didn't want to live in a small growing town, that New York was where she wanted to stay. Her father was not happy with my decision to seek my fortune in the gold fields. But when I asked to marry Rebecca Jane, he agreed but not until after I'd made my fortune. Rebecca Jane agreed, but then when I sent for her, she changed her mind."

"I see. You said you were referred by Mrs. Longworth. Would you mind if I talked to her about you?"

"No. Go ahead. She knows all of this and can confirm what I've said. Do you need directions?"

"No, I passed the sheriff's office on my way here. I thought I'd start there."

"Their home is right next door. You might catch Sam at the office if you want to talk to him as well."

Mr. Lang nodded. "Thank you for your time, Mr. Donovan. I'll give my report to Mrs. Black on my return."

Jesse extended his hand."Thank you, sir. I appreciate it. While you're here would you like to see the rest of the house?"

"Certainly."

Jesse showed him the cook's bedroom

off the kitchen. Then he took him down the hall past the dining room with the solid mahogany table, chairs, buffet and hutch. They passed the parlor with the comfortable looking sofa and overstuffed chairs, all done in a solid blue damask. The curtains were a paisley pattern on a light blue background and there was a blue hued oriental rug in the middle of the room.

They went upstairs to the second floor. Here there were three bedrooms and a bath. The bath had its own small pot-bellied stove to heat the water and there was a pump on the side of the tub.

The bedrooms were furnished, one for a girl with white furniture, one for a boy with dark wood furniture and then the master bedroom. Jesse had the oak bed special made and it was bigger than most regular beds because Jesse was bigger than most men and he was tired of hanging off the end of the bed.

The rooms on the third floor were not furnished.

After he'd seen the entire house, Jesse showed Mr. Lang out. He was fairly sure he'd made a good impression.

*****

May 29, 1873

Clarissa 'Clare' Griggs read the letter from Jesse Donovan to Mrs. Maggie Black again and again. Mrs. Black gave her the missive so Clare could write one back. She hadn't known what to say, but tried her best.

April 10, 1873

Dear Mr. Donovan,
My name is Clarissa Griggs, but most people call me Clare. I am twenty-four years of age, five foot six inches tall with red hair and green eyes. I can cook and keep a home for you. I, too, hope to have many children. I currently live in Golden, Colorado with my parents and four younger siblings. We have a small farm there and everyone helps out. I graduated from high school. The first on both sides of my family to do so.
I am looking forward to meeting you.
Yours truly,
Clare Griggs

She'd been traveling by train and stagecoach for almost eight full days on her way to Hope's Crossing and had worn the same burgundy wool traveling suit under her long black wool coat for the entire trip. Clare hadn't had the time to make a new coat, nor the money to buy one, so hers, though still serviceable, was not in the latest fashion by any means. She wondered if Mr. Jesse Donovan would notice. Clare certainly hoped not.

She'd gathered her wavy hair into a bun on the back of her head and put a black silk scarf over her head and tied it under her chin. The scrap of silk was the nicest thing she owned. She'd saved for over a year to acquire it. Up until this trip, she'd only worn it to church on Sundays. Clare preferred the scarf to a hat because the material helped control her curls. She'd used the rest of her savings, and twenty dollars her parents had given her as a wedding gift to buy material—enough for three dresses, four skirts and five blouses. She could go more than a full week without having to wear the same thing twice. She'd never had so many new clothes in her life. Clare felt like a princess in a fairytale.

The train from Denver to Cheyenne, the first leg of her journey, had been the easiest. She'd been so glad to leave Pa and his attitude. She was never good enough because she wasn't a boy. That was all behind her now and she'd try not to think about it again.

She'd been able to read her book on being a good hostess. Jesse wanted a wife who could be a hostess. She grew up on a farm. What did she know about being a hostess? But her book by Florence Hartley, The Ladies Book of Etiquette and Manual of Politeness would teach her what she needed to know. She hoped that, being a rich man and wanting a wife who could be his hostess, that he had a cook and housekeeper. Just a little dream of hers.

The rest of the trip on the stage from Cheyenne to Hope's Crossing was at best uncomfortable, at worst a nightmare. She'd been jostled against the person next to her when there was only four in the coach. When there were six inside, none of them could move and all were thrilled when they came to a way station and could get out and stretch. The worst part had been that she hadn't been able to read her book at all.

She hoped Mr. Donovan had received her last letter stating she would indeed be coming with the intent to marry. Her arrival would be awkward, to say the least, if he hadn't gotten the note yet. If that was the case, she would stay at the hotel until he was ready to marry her, but he would have to pay for the room. Clare's stomach was tied in knots. She hadn't been able to eat anything at all on this last day of her journey.

All these thoughts about Mr. Donovan not being there or aware of her impending arrival, did nothing to help her stomach. But she couldn't help herself, asking the what if questions.

She certainly couldn't afford to stay at the hotel on her own and if he decided not to marry her at all he would have to buy her ticket back to Golden. The matchmaker, Mrs. Black, had said that sometimes happens but not to worry that she was very sure of this match. Clare didn't understand how she could be so sure, but she seemed so positive, Clare couldn't help but believe her.

When she had been able to sit next to the stagecoach window, she'd seen the same prairie landscape until they got closer to Hope's Crossing. Then they'd gone through the mountains and higher up had even seen snow.

Now the stage was coming into a town

and she was again able to peer out the window as she was the only passenger. The building coming up on the right was tall, maybe the tallest in town. The coach stopped right in front of what turned out to be a hotel.

The shotgun rider opened the door to the stage. "We're here, miss. This is Hope's Crossing."

"Thank you."

Clare exited the stage, picked up her two valises and walked across the boardwalk to the door of the hotel. Three stories all painted yellow with white trim. This was where Mr. Donovan would find her. She looked up and down the street. Both sides of the dirt street were framed by the boardwalk. Here in front of the hotel, the walkway grew to be ten feet wide.

"Miss Griggs?"

The deep baritone voice came from behind her.

She turned and looked up at the devastatingly handsome man with dark brown hair, a well-trimmed mustache, and the most intense brown eyes she'd ever seen. He wore a black wool coat, a black Stetson low on his head, and looked somewhat frightening.

"I'm Clarissa…Clare…Griggs."

He extended his hand. "Jesse Donovan."

She placed her hand in his, and it was immediately swallowed in callused warmth.

"I'm pleased to meet you, Mr. Donovan."

He smiled, showing straight, white teeth.

"If we're to be married, I think you should call me Jesse, and I'll call you Clare."

She smiled unused to speaking with men, much less shaking hands with one. "Yes, of course."

"Are those your bags? Do you have a trunk coming?"

"No, just the bags."

If he thought it strange that she only had the two bags, he didn't say so. He simply picked them both up with one hand and held out his other arm for her to take.

She'd read about men escorting women this way and she put her hand through the crook of his elbow and they walked down the boardwalk together.

"Is your house very far?"

"It's on the outskirts of town. I have my carriage parked next to the hotel on the street just ahead."

They turned the corner and there was a sleek black buggy with matching gray horses hitched in front.

"They're beautiful. I've never seen such a perfect match in a team before." He must really be wealthy, as he told Mrs. Black.

"These two were twins, Very rare. You're familiar with horses?"

"My family has a farm like I mentioned in my letter. I've been around animals all my life."

He placed the bags in the back of the surrey and then helped her onto the seat, after which he walked around and got in the other side next to her.

Hoping she could freshen up a bit before they married, she asked "Are we going to your house now?"

He laughed. "I thought we should get married before I take you home."

She ducked her head, knew she was blushing and chastised herself for her naiveté, then she smiled. "Yes, I suppose that would be best."

"The judge's office is just a couple of blocks this way. Nate is waiting for us. That is the sheriff's office and jail."

He pointed at an unpainted single story building. Bars were on the windows even on the tiny window in the door.

"The sheriff lives next door, in the white house with the small red barn behind it. Sam Longworth is his name. His wife, Jo, was a mail-order bride from Matchmaker & Co., too."

She looked around as he described the buildings.

"So your judge is used to having to marry people in a hurry."

He glanced at her.

"Are you in a hurry to be married, Clare?"

The sensuous tone of his voice caused her to look up at him. He was smiling and a twinkle lit his eyes.

"As a matter of fact, I am. I didn't want to have to stay at the hotel if we are marrying. I want to sleep in my own home."

He lifted an eyebrow.

"In my bed."

CHAPTER 2

Jesse pulled up in front of a one-story brick building. This was the only building she'd seen since arriving in Hope's Crossing, which was made of brick. She guessed that was because it would be too expensive or perhaps it was because of the records kept there and not wanting to lose them in a fire.

"This is the courthouse. The judge's offices are inside."

They walked up the three steps to the white double doors and entered onto a long hallway with offices on both sides. About half way down the corridor, Jesse stopped in front of a door and took a breath. The sign said Nathaniel J. Harden, Justice of the

Peace.

Jessie stepped into the outer office of the judge's chambers. There was a tall counter with a swinging gate. At a desk behind the counter sat a scrawny young man with blond hair and glasses.

"Can you please tell the judge that Jesse Donovan is here to see him?" Jesse asked the young man.

"Yes, sir." He left and walked through a door that was ajar and returned quickly.

"I'm coming," said a gravelly voice from the inner office.

A few moments later a rotund man with gray beard and hair, pulling on his black robes, emerged from the back office.

"Well, Jesse. Is this lovely lady the one you're marrying?"

He eased Clare forward.

"She sure is, Nate. Are you ready to do the honors?"

"Clarence," said the judge to the young man at the desk. "Take down the information for the marriage license."

"Yes, sir," answered Clarence from his desk, paper and pen in hand.

"What are your full names?" asked Judge Hardin.

"Jesse Eugene Donovan."

"Clarissa Mae Griggs." She spelled her names for him so they would be sure and be correct on the marriage license.

"Got that, Clarence?"

"Yes, sir, your honor. I'll get the license filled out right away."

"First," said the judge. "Go get Sarah. She can be the second witness."

"Be right back," the young man said as he hurried out the door.

"She's just in the next office over, they'll return shortly," said Nate. "Come into my chambers and we'll have the ceremony in there."

No sooner had they gotten into the judges office when the door opened and Clarence returned with a young blonde woman wearing spectacles. Clare looked over at Jesse to see if he noticed her. He didn't seem to pay any attention.

"Good afternoon, Nate," said Sarah.

"It's Your Honor," hissed Clarence.

"It's Nate," insisted Sarah. "He's my father's best friend and I've known him all my life."

"Shh. Both of you," said the judge with a shake of his head. "Let's get this wedding over and then you can go back to arguing after that."

Both of them looked mutinous but they hushed.

The quibbling between Clarence and Sarah provided Clare the time she needed to settle her nerves. She was ready for this. She squared her shoulders and took a breath.

"Jesse, you and Clare stand in front of me, right here." He pointed to a spot about three feet away from him. "Clarence and Sarah, you stand next to them. You know where to stand. You've both done this enough."

Clarence stood on Jesse's right and Sarah on Clare's left.

"Now. We are gathered together in front of these witnesses to join this man and this woman in holy matrimony. Do you Clarissa Mae Griggs, take this man to be your lawful wedded husband, to have and to hold, in sickness and in health, for richer or for poorer, and to keep yourself only unto him, for as long as you both shall live?"

Clare looked up at Jesse and swallowed hard before whispering, "I do."

"Do you Jesse Eugene Donovan, take this woman to be your lawful wedded wife, to have and to hold, in sickness and in health, for richer or for poorer, and to keep yourself only unto her, for as long as you both shall live?"

"I do." Jesse said clearly in his rich baritone she was learning to like very much.

"Jesse, do you have a ring?"

"I do, Your Honor."

He put a diamond and gold band on the third finger of her left hand.

"Now repeat after me. With this ring, I thee wed."

"With this ring, I thee wed." Jesse looked at her and smiled when he finished.

"By the power vested in me by the Town of Hope's Crossing and the Territory of Montana, I now pronounce you man and wife. You may kiss your bride."

Jesse leaned in and pressed his lips against hers. She started to pull back, his mustache tickled, but he held her head and deepened the kiss, pressing his tongue forward until she opened, then he devoured her, leaving her tingling all over and wanting more. For her first kiss, it was amazing.

Finally he stood back and smiled.

"You'll do Mrs. Donovan. You'll

definitely do."

She saw the twinkle in those brown eyes that were now the color of warm brandy and wondered what he saw in her that made him smile.

Clare raised her eyebrows. "I guess you'll do as well, Mr. Donovan." She turned her gaze to her ring. Gold and diamonds, probably worth more than her daddy's farm, blazed from her finger. She couldn't help but admire it.

"Well then, if you'll both sign here, we'll be done and you're free to go." The judge put the license on the counter and Clare and Jesse both signed it.

"Thanks, Nate."

Jesse put a twenty dollar double eagle gold piece in the judges hand.

"You're welcome," said the judge. "See you at the poker game tomorrow?"

Jesse looked at Clare and that intense look was back.

"Afraid I'll be busy tomorrow night."

*****

Jesse escorted Clare from the courthouse and back to the carriage. He helped her in and then got in beside her and slapped the reins on the horses butts to get them moving.

He wanted her in the worst way. Her gorgeous red hair spread beneath her on the bed, him over her…

"Jesse. Jesse?"

He shook his head, clearing it and saw Clare snap her fingers in front of his face.

"Sorry. Had my mind elsewhere."

She cocked an eyebrow.

"Must have been someplace pretty special for you not to hear me."

"Oh, it was." He smiled and glanced down at her. "Now what did you need? You have my full attention."

"I wondered if we could talk about our…wedding night."

She blushed so prettily.

"What about it?"

"I think we need to get to know each other first."

"What difference does that make now? We're married, for better or worse."

She wrung her reticule in her hands.

"I know but if we could just wait a couple of weeks—"

"No," he said softly, shaking his head.

"But Jesse."

He sighed and turned in the seat toward her. "What's really the problem? Getting to know each other for two weeks won't change anything."

"Fine. I'm scared Jesse. I grew up on a farm. I know how it all works and I know there will be pain and—"

"Don't be afraid." He looked at her and set his hand on her knee. "I'll do my best to prepare you before, so the pain won't be so bad."

Her eyes were wide with fear. That wasn't good. A frigid bride, too scared to enjoy anything, was not what he wanted.

"Tell you what. I'll give you a couple of days to get used to me. For us to get used to being around each other. We will sleep together, but I promise I won't make love to you. Will that work?"

"Oh, yes." Clare smiled wide. "Thank you. I appreciate it. You'll see everything will be better."

"That is my hope. Now let's go home and I'll show you around the property."

"Tell me about your home. Do you have animals? Can I have a kitten? Do you want a dog? Do you—"

"Whoa. Hold on. One question at a time."

Clare laughed.

The sound was deep, smoky and made him want to grab her up and kiss her.

"I do have animals. I have a big barn behind the house with a couple of milk cows and six horses. I have a chicken coop with about fifteen chickens and the cockiest rooster you'll ever meet. I already have a dog, name of Smokey, and yes, you can have a kitten. We have barn cats and they have kittens all the time. You can pick one out of the current litter."

"Oh, thank you, Jesse."

She smiled and he saw she had the greenest eyes, sparkling with happiness.

"I had a cat back home that I couldn't bring. I even know what I'm naming the new one. Jasper."

"What if you pick out a girl kitten? Jasper is a boy's name."

"Well, then I guess that kitten will just have to get used to having a boy's name."

It was his turn to laugh. His bride was a refreshing change to what Rebecca Jane had been. All she had cared about was position and power. How many people she could lord over that she was the best, at…whatever. The prettiest girl at the party, on the arm of the most handsome man, she didn't care as long as she thought she was better than everyone else. Jesse often wondered what attracted him to such a woman, initially it was her beauty, but he found beneath her greedy exterior, was a heart that cared about family. Her family was important to her, just as his was important to him.

That was why he'd waited until he struck it rich to ask her to marry him. When she found out how much he was worth, she said yes. But it turned out even the money wasn't enough to make her leave New York.

"What are you thinking about so hard?"

"Huh? What? I'm sorry I was thinking how different you are than my former fiancée."

"Were you very much in love with her?"

Clare blushed and looked down at her lap, while she wrung her reticule in her hands. A nervous habit he'd noticed.

"No. I was not very much in love with her. I thought I was, but I was wrong."

"What makes you think you were wrong?"

"I think her not coming out here would have hurt, or at least hurt more, if I'd really been in love with her."

"You weren't hurt by her shameful

decision?"

"No, I was angry. But I quickly got over my anger and simply put in for a replacement bride from Matchmaker & Co and here you are."

"Yes, here I am."

He heard the sadness in her voice and was sorry he put it there by calling her a replacement bride, even though that's what she was, he was sorry he'd hurt her.

"Don't sound so forlorn. The situation we find ourselves in is one of great opportunity. We can create a dynasty right here in this little valley. Our children and grandchildren will be raised in Hope's Crossing. We'll build a school and after they've learned all they can here, they can then go to college."

Her gaze was wide and she seemed surprised. "You're quite passionate about this."

"I'm quite passionate about many things."

They were at the end of Main Street and there were no buildings, no people to censure them. He put the reins in one hand and used the other to wrap around her waist and bring her close. Then he slanted his lips over hers and this time when he pushed with his tongue she let him in immediately, seemingly as anxious to taste him as he was to taste her.

She wrapped her arms around his neck and pressed her chest to his and then kissed him. Clare was a quick learner; Rebecca Jane had never kissed him like this.

He finally pulled back and grinned at her.

"I hope those two days pass fast, because I can hardly wait to make love to you."

Red as a radish, she looked in her lap and didn't say a word.

He laughed, liking that he could cause that reaction.

He pulled onto the long driveway that led to his house. As they got closer, he watched her eyes grow wider.

"How do you like it?" The little boy in him felt the need for her approval.

"The house is beautiful as are the grounds that I can see."

"I'm glad you like it. I'll take you inside, and then I'll have to take care of the horses."

He came around to her side of the buggy and helped her down.

After she was on the ground, she pressed her hands across her skirt

Jesse held out his arm, and she put her hand daintily through the crook of his elbow. Together, they walked up the red stone path to the porch of the three story blue house with white trim.

Three steps led up to a wide veranda. A rail edged the porch and the roof was held up by white columns every eight or ten feet.

"Oh, Jesse. You put up a swing. How wonderful." Clare let go of his arm, walked over to the swing and sat, trying it out.

He smiled remembering that was Jo's suggestion. Sam had followed suit and built a porch onto his house wide enough to have a swing and a couple of rockers.

"Would you like to see the rest of the house?"

"Oh, of course. I'm sorry. I'm easily distracted sometimes."

"That's all right." He held open the screened door for her to pass through.

*****

Clare walked through the door into a home more beautiful than she could have imagined. They entered the living room with stairs on the right side. Jesse had decorated very nicely. She wondered if he'd done it himself or had help. The walls were painted above and papered below a chair rail. The paint was a pale cream color and the background of the wallpaper was also cream, but full of small vines with blue flowers. The comfortable looking sofa, upholstered in a lovely dark blue material and the overstuffed chairs, covered in blue brocade, were around a coffee table and encouraged conversation. She couldn't have arranged them better herself.

The fireplace against the far wall was made of the same red stone as the path outside and was the focal point of the room.

"What is that red stone? I've never seen anything like it."

"It is called flag-stone. Do you like it?"

"Oh, yes. Very much."

A window was on the wall behind the sofa, and bookshelves were built in to the wall on the last side.

"This room is beautifully decorated. You did this alone?"

"For the most part. I had Jo and Effie help me on the colors."

"Effie?"

So many new people she'd be meeting,

would she ever remember all their names?

Jesse smiled. "She's the little old lady who runs the hotel and post office. And she has an opinion about everything. You'll meet her soon. Ready to see the rest of the house?"

Clare can hardly believe that she is really going to live here in this beautiful house. "Oh, yes, please, if you don't mind."

"Of course, not. This is your home now."

He took her past the dining room, where a large mahogany table and chairs stood, on to the kitchen. Here especially, she could tell he'd designed it with a wife in mind. There were long counters with cupboards above and both cupboards and drawers below. A pump sat on one side of the sink, so she didn't have to go outside to get water.

A long table with six chairs was along the wall across from the counters. The door to the outside was on the wall to her left, and through the window in the door she saw a clothes line in the back yard.

The largest stove she'd ever seen, with a full six burners, was on her right. The stove had an oven, a chamber for wood or coal under the burners, and a warming shelf above the burners. The doors and handles were all ceramic, painted a lovely blue-green. On that same wall was another door she thought must go to the pantry. A large two door icebox was about four feet from the sink with counter in-between.

"I don't know how much more I can take. The house is so perfect. I could have designed it myself."

Jesse beamed.

Clearly pleased by her remarks.

"There's a bedroom for the housekeeper through there." He pointed at a door in the wall at the end of the table.

"Do we have a housekeeper?"

She hoped she kept the desire out of her voice.

"No. I don't need one now. I have you."

"Oh." She closed her eyes and let her dream die a little. It didn't matter. She was used to hard work; she just wasn't sure how she'd be able to clean this big house by herself and do the laundry and the cooking and be a good hostess.

They walked back down the hall to the stairs and climbed to the second floor.

"There are three bedrooms here and three on the floor above us. I haven't furnished the ones up there yet." He pointed at the ceiling.

Clare raised an eyebrow. "I'm sure there's plenty of time to get furniture in those rooms before they are needed." Good grief six bedrooms to clean. How am I suppose to do all this and cook and hostess?

He chuckled. "Yes, I suppose there is."

The two smaller bedrooms were furnished alike. Bed, dresser, bureau, and commode. One with white furniture and one with dark wood furnishings, as though one was for a boy and one for a girl.

The master suite was magnificent. A large four-poster wooden bed made of what looked like solid oak dominated the room. All the furniture in this room was of the same light wood. The four-drawer bureau had two large drawers as wide as the bureau. On top of those were two smaller drawers only half the width of the larger drawers. Jesse had left one small one and one large drawer empty for her. My clothes won't fill one of the small drawers much less a large one. She did love the mirror that ran the length of the bureau was attached to the back. Next to the dresser was a tall chest of drawers with the top drawer left empty for her.

He'd purchased a beautiful Chinese screen behind which were the chamber pot and the commode. The pitcher, sitting atop the commode, had a Chinese motif that matched the folding screen. The urn was one of the prettiest pieces of ceramic she'd ever seen.

"This room is lovely. Surely, you had help with its decoration."

"A little." He hesitated and then admitted. "This is how the furniture was shown in the catalog I ordered it from."

She smiled and nodded. "Now that makes sense."

"What? You didn't think I could do this," he waved his arm around the room. "Alone?"

"No. I didn't. Most men are not that concerned with decorating the house."

"I was doing it with my bride in mind."

Clare bowed her head and looked at the floor. "Yes, I know. Rebecca Jane."

"That is true. I was designing this house to be something that I thought she would like. I should have known better," he said bitterly.

She looked up at him and even though

she'd expected his answer, it still hurt just a little that everything was done for someone else, but what else had she expected?

"I'm sorry you were hurt, but I can't say I'm sorry she backed out for if she had not I wouldn't be here."

Jesse stopped and took her hands in his and brought them around his waist, then he wrapped her in his arms.

"Are you glad you're here? Not sorry you married me?"

"No. I'm not sorry." She lifted one brow. "At least not yet."

"Good."

He pulled her close and touched his lips to hers, lightly and then full on, taking her breath away.

CHAPTER 3

"Do you know how much I want to take you to bed and have my way with you?"

"I can imagine." She shuddered, remembering that there was pain involved with coupling. "But you already said I could have a couple of days and I know you won't go back on your word."

"What makes you think that?"

She leaned back in his arms to look up into his coffee brown eyes, so dark now as to be almost black.

"Because I think that is what hurt you more than anything with Rebecca Jane. She went back on her promise to marry you. She didn't keep her word."

Jesse eased his hold on her, his hands

lingering on her waist before finally setting her free. They stood in the master bedroom, with that bed laughing at her for her fear.

"You're an astute woman Clare Donovan. Yes, that is what hurt. I had no delusions that she might love me, at least not right away. Rebecca Jane is too conceited to love anyone other than herself. But I'd hoped if I loved her enough, she'd change her mind and love me back, silly fool that I was."

"But I suppose she was beautiful." She cringed at the resignation and jealousy she heard in her voice.

"Yes, she is. About your height, blonde hair, blue eyes, though not as curvaceous as you. I find I like your curves."

Clare felt the heat in her cheeks. "I'm glad because they are not going anywhere."

"Good. Now would you like to see the barn and pick out a kitten?"

She was thankful for the change in subject and bounced on the balls of her feet, grinning. "Oh, yes. Very much."

They walked across the yard toward the outbuilding. Very big and painted red, there was no way it could be anything else but the barn.

Inside were ten stalls. Horses occupied six of those, cows two, one was empty and the last one held hay, straw, and many, many cats and kittens. They lay on the bales and on top of each other in piles on the floor. They rolled around on the straw battling with each other in play and one, a little black-and-white one, walked right up to Jesse and rubbed against him. The kitten then came over to Clare and did the same to her.

That was all she needed.

"This one." She stooped and picked up the little cat.

"That's a runt, it probably won't get very big."

"I don't care. Look how he rubbed against us. He knows. He already loves us." She rubbed her nose against the baby cat's. "Yes, you do. And I love you, too."

Jesse shook his head. "I should have known. That little kitten has been following me every time I come into the barn."

Clare smiled. "He knew I was coming and was getting you used to the idea of having a tiny panther running around the house."

"Anywhere but the bed. The cat is not

allowed in the bed with us."

Clare looked away and down into the kitten's face. "Of course." Then she whispered to the cat. "We'll see."

She looked up at Jesse through her lashes and saw him smiling and shaking his head.

He had heard her, but he wasn't angry. That was a good start to their marriage.

She took the kitten to the house and sat him on the bed while she checked for room for her clothes. Jesse had left room in the closet and the top dresser drawer. He also emptied one large and one small bureau drawer for her use. Clare didn't need all that room now, but was pleased that he'd thought to leave her so much.

"Clare." Jesse's deep, rich baritone rolled over her like waves of her favorite chocolate.

She turned to look at him. "What can I do for you?"

Standing with his arms folded over his chest, he jutted his chin toward the bed.

Jasper had made himself a bed on one of the pillows.

"I bet that pillow's yours, isn't it?"
He nodded.

"He must smell you on it. I can't help that he loves you."

Jesse rolled his eyes. "He's a cat. He doesn't feel love."

"Of course, he does. He's got a heart and a brain just like the rest of us. Why couldn't he love you?" She stepped closer, letting the skirt in her hand hang at her side. "Even if you're right, and I'm not saying you are, he still recognizes your scent and the odor soothes him."

Jesse sighed and shook his head. "Let's hope it soothes you, too." He pushed away from the door. "I've got chores to do. I'll be back in time for dinner at six o'clock. I also thought I should let you know that we're hosting our first dinner party on Saturday."

A gasp escaped. "Saturday! That's just two days from now. How many are coming? What do you want me to prepare?"

Suddenly her stomach hurt. She'd never be able to pull this off. First she only had one dress that was nice enough for a dinner party, second he expected her to cook and be the hostess, too. Her book didn't tell her how to do that.

Jesse walked over and took her by the shoulders.

"Calm down. We'll discuss the situation over dinner."

Then he leaned down and kissed her.

"Trust me."

Clare took a deep breath, let it out and nodded. "At dinner."

"Yes. I know there are a couple of steaks in the icebox. Check out the pantry for whatever else you need. Now, I really have to go. The animals are waiting."

"Go." She shooed him away waving her arms in front of her. "I'll be fine and I'll have dinner ready by six."

"All right see you then."

He turned and left the room.

The clock on the bureau showed the time to be three o'clock. She'd better unpack and then figure out what to fix with those steaks for dinner. Clare hung her dresses, skirts and shirtwaists in the closet. She folded her chemises and bloomers and put them in the large bureau drawer. Then she folded her nightgown and robe and put them in the dresser drawer.

When she was done she picked up Jasper, who meowed at being disturbed and took the kitten with her to the kitchen. There was a tall-sided box full of wood next to the stove. Clare emptied it, cleaned it out, put a couple of towels in the bottom and put Jasper in the box. The sides were tall enough that he couldn't jump out yet.

He meowed pitifully when she straightened.

"Hush, now. It's just temporary. I don't want to step on you while I'm cooking."

She rummaged through the cupboards until she found the saucers, filled one with milk and put it in the box with the little cat.

Jasper took to the milk right away, and after he finished the full saucer, lay down in the corner of the box for a nap.

Oh, to be a kitten with nothing to do but eat and sleep and play.

"I see you found a box for the kitten."

Clare jumped and turned in surprise toward Jesse. "Don't sneak up on me like that?"

He put his hands up. "I wasn't sneaking. You were simply too enamored with your baby cat to hear me. And I'm not used to having to announce myself when I enter a room. I've been living alone for a long time."

She took a deep breath and nodded. "I'm sorry. You're right, I am captivated by him.

I think he's adorable."

"Women." Jesse shook his head. "I've got the milk for today you'll need to—"

"I know, strain it through cheese cloth, put it in the new milk can ready for the ice house." She paused and tried to remember the out buildings she'd seen. "Do we have an icehouse? The icebox won't hold these milk cans."

"We don't have an ice house. I sell it to Smith's Mercantile. When you have it strained and ready to go, let me know and I'll take the milk to the store."

"Why do you sell milk to the store? You're rich. You don't need the money."

"I've always done it and I can't stand the thought of the milk going to waste and having to throw it away."

"I understand that. If you'll let me freshen up and change clothes, I'll go with you to the store. I need to get to know these people."

She got the cheese cloth out and strained the milk into a clean milk can.

"All right. I'll introduce you around."

"Thank you, I appreciate that. I need to pick up some food stuffs at the store. Do you have a scrap of paper and a pencil so I can make a list?"

Jesse rummaged around in one of the drawers in the kitchen and came back with the items.

"Now let's see. We need more canned goods, potatoes, flour, sugar, cocoa powder, cinnamon…"

He frowned and scratched his jaw. "What do you need all that stuff for?"

"I need them to cook and to bake." This was the way her mother ran her household and she always thought it was the right way, but maybe Jesse had other ideas. "Don't you like sweets and fresh bread?"

"Like them?" His eyes got wide and he smiled. "I love them but I don't get fresh bread or dessert unless I go out to eat."

"Well, you do now."

Jesse rubbed his hands together. "I can't wait. Do you want to go to the store now? I still haven't unhitched the buggy."

"Give me just a couple of minutes to freshen up. I've been in these clothes for eight days straight and don't want to meet your friends smelling like a farm animal."

"All right. Go ahead. I'll go give the horses some water and load the milk into the back."

She was back quickly. "Let's go." She'd changed into a pink shirtwaist with a black wool skirt and washed her face, neck and hands. Clare felt ever so much better.

Jesse held the door open for her and then took her hand and hooked it around his arm as they walked. When they reached the surrey, he helped her up.

"Thank you. You're such the gentleman."

"That's the way I was raised. You look quite lovely and definitely refreshed. I'll see about getting you a bath tonight."

"Thank you, that will be much appreciated. You were raised right, you know. I intend to do the same for our children. Raise them to be polite men and women. Where did you grow up?"

"I was the eldest of eight children and grew up on a farm in Missouri. We were dirt poor. When Pa died, I left so as not to be another burden on my mother and went to New York City. I made some money, met Rebecca Jane. Then I decided, New York was not the life for me. I needed the open spaces, so I came out here and bought a mining claim. Lucky for me it was a good one. Now I can take care of my siblings and my mother."

"Have you thought of having your mother come here to live with us?"

Jesse stopped walking and turned to look at her.

"You would do that? Have my mother in the same house?"

What an odd thing to say. "Of course, she's your mother."

"That's very nice of you. I'll have to get in touch with her and see if she would like to come up here. Thank you, Clare."

"You don't need to thank me. It's the right thing to do."

The trip to the mercantile took only about five minutes. The building was located between the hotel and the butcher shop on the west side of the town. A single story, red building with white trim around the windows and white double doors, the store was quite inviting.

"Miss Smith," Jesse called as they entered the store with the milk can.

"Be right there," came a woman's voice from the back.

Soon a very short woman with snow white hair, wearing a bright blue dress with an apron over it, rushed up to them.

"Jesse, good to see you, boy, and you have my milk. Good, good. I need to get it into the bottles right away and into the icebox." She turned to Clare. "And who do we have here? Will you introduce me to your lovely lady?"

"Clare Donovan. Please meet Lavernia Smith. She and Effie are sisters."

"Pleased to—"

"Don't mention that woman to me," Lavernia spat.

"What's the matter now?"

The way Jesse said it, with a roll of his eyes, told Clare this happened a lot.

"You might as well tell me," coaxed Jesse with a wide smile.

"That woman is telling people that I'm six years older than she is and it's not true. She and I are the same age. We're twins, but I arrived earlier by thirty-two seconds, and she's never gotten over that."

"Twins? That explains a lot," said Jesse. "We always thought you two looked an awful lot alike, but Miss Effie wears her bun high on her head and you wear it low. That's how we tell you apart."

"There is a reason for that, young Jesse. The very reason you mention. She used to copy whatever I was doing so we looked alike. I finally cut my hair. Well, she wasn't about to cut hers, she's always been real proud of her hair. So she puts her hair up in the high knot. I keep mine shorter so it can only go in the low knot. But enough of that." She waved her hand in front of her. "Did I hear you say Clare Donovan? Your…sister?"

"Nope. Wife. Got married this morning."

Clare looked over at Jesse and smiled. The rivalry between Lavernia and Effie, reminded her of her own sister, June, who was only a year younger than Clare and always trying to prove she was the best at everything. Including marriage. June had married her childhood sweetheart last year and was now expecting their first child.

"Well now," said Lavernia. "That's wonderful, just wonderful. I'll put all her purchases on your tab. What can I do for you today?"

"I've got a list of things I need. Jesse wasn't one for baking much and I love to. I intend to bake all our bread, pies, cakes, cookies, everything."

"If you ever have too much, bring your

baked goods in here. They would sell like hotcakes."

The elderly woman grinned at her pun.

"We got lots of single men who don't cook much less bake." Lavernia went on. "In case you haven't been here long enough to notice, we got very few women here in Hope's Crossing. Heck, even Effie and I get marriage proposals now and again." She cackled

"I doubt she'll have any leftovers," said Jesse. "I've got me a mighty big sweet tooth."

Lavernia laughed. "So you do."

Clare followed Lavernia through the store and picked up all the things on her list. She was even able to get the cinnamon, which surprised her. Back home whenever her pa had enough money for spices he'd always ordered them special.

Jesse loaded everything into the buggy, then he and Clare walked to the next shop which was the butcher. The building was painted white with brown shutters and door.

Clare didn't know if it was because Hope's Crossing was a relatively new town, it was different than her hometown of Golden, Colorado.

"Is there some reason that every building in town has recently been painted?"

"Not really other than the fact that they hadn't been painted before. Everything was just wood. As we grow into a real town, painting seemed…appropriate."

"How old is the town?"

"I've been here for three years. It was just tents then."

"Painting as the town grows makes sense."

Jesse raised his eyebrows. "I'm glad you think so."

"I didn't mean it in a bad way."

Jesse smiled. "I know. I'm teasing you."

They walked into the butcher shop. The man behind the counter came out to greet them.

"Jesse. I gots de roast you vanted."

"Great." Jesse put his arm around Clare's waist. "Klaus Rhineberg, this is my wife, Clare. Klaus is our friendly butcher. You tell him when and what you need and he'll get it for you. If you don't know what you want, ask and he'll suggest things and he's a font of recipes for meat."

"Wonderful." Clare shook Mr. Rhineberg's hand. The portly, German man was quite jovial. He wore a long apron over his clothes that hung nearly to his shoes. Probably in his mid-forties, he had brown hair and a full beard and mustache.

Mr. Rhineberg put a huge package on the counter.

"That's the roast you ordered? What in the world is that for?" Clare asked as Jesse hefted the package from the counter. "How much does that weigh?"

"It's for our dinner party on Saturday? Did you forget already? And it weighs close to twelve pounds."

"Twelve pounds!" Her stomach roiled. How would she ever pull this off. "How many people do you have coming to this party?"

"Just a few. Sam and Jo will be there, and the other mine owners with their wives, if they have them. Only about four of them have wives. It's kind of hard to get women to come to a mining town."

She tilted her head. "So I understand. Now, how many people all together?"

"About twenty."

"Twenty. Twenty for dinner." The cupboard with the dishes flashed in her mind and she wondered if there were enough place settings. "I won't bore Mr. Rhineberg with our squabbles."

The side of Jesse's mouth quirked up and he narrowed his eyes before shrugging. "All right. Thanks Klaus. See you soon."

"Ya, ya tank you very much."

Clare walked out in front of Jesse and held the butcher shop door for him so it would not slam.

They walked to where the buggy remained parked in front of the mercantile. Jesse put the roast in the back with the rest of the groceries and then helped Clare into the vehicle.

"Now will you tell me what has put a bee in your bonnet?" asked Jesse as he climbed in next to her.

"You're having twenty people over for a meal on Saturday and I'm only given two days to prepare?"

"I thought that would be enough. I want everyone to meet my new bride."

Jesse put his hand on her knee.

With a two-fingered grasp, she moved it back to his leg.

"It's barely enough. At least you thought to have the food ordered. Now, what else do you want with this roast?"

He shook his head. "I don't know. Should I remind you that I asked for a bride who could handle this and that in your letter you said you could cook?"

"No, you should not. No woman in the world would be happy with only two days to prepare for a large dinner party, I don't care how much they know."

Clare closed her eyes and pinched the skin between them. "Very well. I saw that you had potatoes, so I can make mashed potatoes and gravy. I bought canned green beans, peas, beets and carrots. That was all they had and I think I cleaned them out. What vegetables would you like?"

"Peas and carrots."

"Good choices, they'll be colorful. I'll bake bread and a cake tomorrow or would you rather have a pie. I got some canned cherries."

"I'd like a yellow cake with chocolate icing or a cherry pie."

"The pie is easier, so I'll do that."

"Why did you ask?"

"So I can get your preferences. I assume with a home like yours that you don't plan on this being the last party, that you can afford more than one."

He chuckled. "Yes, I can afford more than one party."

"Good. The next party, I'll have more time, and by then you will have hired a cook."

"What? Why should I hire a cook? I have you."

"Because I can't properly hostess your party and cook it, too. Of course, perhaps you'd rather that I just cook and you can hire a hostess."

He rolled his eyes. "All right I'll hire a housekeeper and cook."

"Who do you use now? Perhaps she'd consider both positions."

He nodded slowly. "You know, she just might. Being around people would be good for her. She lost her husband in a mine accident and has been alone now for several years. Her name is Nora."

"Drop me and the food off at the house and then go see if Nora is willing to come right away."

Jesse grinned. "Yes, ma'am, Mrs. Donovan. Whatever you need."

CHAPTER 4

"Clare," Jesse called from the door. "Clare. We're back."

Clare came out of the kitchen, holding her kitten, Jasper. She went directly to the woman who was only about ten years older. She was quite lovely with her dark, almost black hair and deep blue eyes.

Jesse followed Nora with her bags.

"I'm Clare Donovan," She extended her hand. "I'm so happy to meet you."

"Nora Daniels, glad to meet you, too."

"And this is Jasper." She petted the kitten.

Nora reached over and petted the little cat, which was so comfortable in Clare's arms that he purred.

"Shall we get you settled in your room?

Then you can help me plan this dinner party that my new husband has decided we're having on Saturday night."

Clare turned to walk toward the kitchen and the nearby bedroom.

"Didn't give you any warning, huh?" asked Nora.

"We just got married this morning, and he tells me about this right after we get home from the ceremony. Can you imagine?"

Nora shook her dark head. "What was he thinking?"

"I'm right here, ladies. You don't have to talk about me as though I'm not in the room."

Jesse followed behind them carrying Nora's two carpet bags.

"We're ignoring you," said Clare. "You've given us enough trouble for one day."

"Look, I didn't think this dinner would be such a big deal. Just a few friends in for supper."

"A few friends?" asked Clare with her hands fisted on her hips. "The sheriff and other mine owners? That's not a few friends—this is a business dinner regardless of what you choose to call the meal."

Jesse ran his hand behind his neck. "Well, yes, I guess it is. I want to make a good impression on everyone here, because I'm thinking about asking them to support me for mayor."

Clare blinked several times. "You want to ask them what? Don't you think that is something we should have talked about before I came?"

"What is wrong with being a mayor's wife?" Jesse asked. "Besides, I mentioned it in the letter I sent. Did you actually read my letter?"

"Of course, I did. Several times. You did not mention running for mayor, just that you needed a hostess. People have a certain expectation of what the mayor's wife should be and I'm not it. They want someone who is fashionable and is considered to have good breeding." She waved her hand at her simple shirtwaist and skirt. "I'm just a farmer's daughter."

"Don't sell yourself short, Clare. You seem to be a bright young woman. You had Jesse come hire me full time." said Nora with a smile.

Clare smiled back. "Thank you. That's

very kind of you to say."

"Not at all. I call 'em as I see 'em," replied Nora.

They walked through the kitchen into the bedroom. Jesse had furnished it with a lovely curved and curly brass framed double bed. On the bed was a white lace coverlet and the window curtain was matching lace but dyed pale blue. He'd bought white furniture, a bureau with small attached mirror, chest of drawers and commode.

"Oh my," said Nora. "Is this special place to be my room?"

"Sure." Jesse set the two bags on the bed. "You don't like it?"

Tears filled Nora's eyes and she turned to Clare, who stood behind her.

"I've never seen a place so lovely. Thank you."

Clare wrapped her arms around the older woman's shoulders.

"Don't cry. I'm glad you like your room and am so very happy you're here. Now, unpack your things and meet me in the kitchen," she said with a deep voice and squared shoulders.

"Yes ma'am," replied Nora.

"I'm Clare and he's Jesse. There'll be no

ma'am and sir in this house."

"Fine by me," said Nora.

"Jesse, let's go and give her some privacy."

Clare waved her arms and shooed Jesse out of the room.

She found a piece of paper and a pencil in one of the drawers, and then she and Jesse sat at the kitchen table.

"Tell me the names of these people you have coming."

"Well, there's Sheriff Sam Longworth and his wife, Jo. Mine owners Rich and Bonnie Heidger, Robert and Kate Morse, Ezra and Florence Sharecroft, Will and Phyllis Nelson, Jonas Taylor, Curt Ames, Ed Regan, and Gabe Swanson. All of them have mines around Hope's Crossing and miners working for them."

Clare madly wrote down all the names so she could try and memorize them. The night of the party she would then be able to put faces with names.

"Are they all friends or are there those we should keep apart?"

"No, we're all good friends."

"Are you sure that roast will be enough? Perhaps we should do a ham, too. I don't want anyone to walk away from our table hungry"

"That won't happen."

"I want to make sure." She put the end of the pencil in her mouth and thought for a moment. "Would you pick up a ham from the butcher tomorrow? A five pound one should do the trick."

"Sure. But I don't think it's necessary."

"Perhaps not, but if there are leftovers, we'll simply be eating them for a week."

Nora entered from her bedroom. Clare saw that her eyes were a little red and puffy. She'd cried over the beautiful room. Not that Clare blamed her. This house was the prettiest she'd ever seen.

Jesse had put a lot of money and thought into furnishing the house, even if it was just a copy of what he saw in the catalog.

"Would you get us all some coffee, Nora. There's a fresh pot." She nodded toward the stove.

"Do you need me for anything else?" asked Jesse.

"Not right now, but I'll probably have more questions as we get closer to Saturday."

"Then after I gather the eggs, I'm

headed up to the mine. I need to get my daily reports from my managers."

Jesse got up and ambled out of the room.

Nora came to the table with two china cups of coffee. Jesse had spared no expense and had china rather than simple ceramic or tin dishes.

Clare took a cup, blew on the liquid inside and sipped the hot brew. "Thanks. Which cupboard are the cups in?"

"To the right of the sink, next to the icebox."

"We may want to rearrange the kitchen at some point in the future. I'm sure Jesse won't mind."

"By that time, you'll be used to the placement of everything and won't need to change it."

Clare sighed. "That's probably true. So, this is what I've planned for the dinner on Saturday. I've got a beef roast and Jesse is picking up a ham tomorrow. We have potatoes and canned vegetables for side dishes and I'll bake fresh bread and make several cherry pies for dessert."

"Sounds like you have everything under control. What do you want me to do?"

"What has your schedule been here?

When is the last time you were in to clean the house? It looks very clean to me, but I'd like to go over everything down here again before the party so there's not a speck of dust anywhere."

"I used to come in once a week on Fridays, so cleaning again before the party is right on my schedule."

Clare nodded. "This party has me rattled and I don't want Jesse to know how totally inadequate I feel. I just got married, I don't have any idea who these people are and I want to make a good impression."

Nora laughed. "You're doing fine. I know most of those people and they are just folks like you and me. They weren't rich before they struck gold and with the exception of the Nelson's, who can be a bit uppity, they're still just regular people."

"I hope you're right. I don't want Jesse to be embarrassed by me."

"I won't be, regardless of how this supper turns out."

Jesse walked in from the outside, holding a basket of eggs in his hand.

Clare was happy that he had confidence in her, still she had doubt.

"How can you say that? I could be the

laughing stock of the town when this is done."

"No. You can't. That job is already taken."

She frowned. "You're just trying to be funny."

He put his hand on her shoulder.

"No, I'm not. That job is taken by an old man by the name of Dirty Barney Finkle."

Jesse grinned.

Nora chuckled and shook her head.

Clare began to laugh. First just a little giggle, then a chuckle and then a full blown laugh.

"I'm being silly, aren't I?"

"Just a little." Jesse put the basket of eggs on the counter.

"These people are my friends. I want them to like you, but more importantly I want you to like them. Can't you just consider this the after-wedding party, just a couple of days late?"

"Sure." Clare, happy that he wanted his friends to like her, gave a little nod. "I can do that."

"Great. Now you've got everything settled with Nora, and she'll get our supper for tonight started, won't you, please Nora?"

"Yes, sir…I mean Jesse. I saw those steaks in the icebox. I'll fry 'em up with some potatoes and make a pan of biscuits to go with them."

"Open one of those cans of beets, please. They're my favorite," said Clare. She thought about how her life had changed in just a day. She'd gone from a poor farm girl to married, with a housekeeper so she didn't even have to do the basic chores anymore. And she was becoming the hostess, like she'd read in her book.

The steaks were huge. She and Nora split one steak with plenty of meat for each of them, and Jesse had the other. Dinner was quick and delicious. If Nora's biscuits weren't the best she'd ever had, Clare would eat her hat.

Now though she stood looking at her bed. Dinner was done, the dishes were cleaned, she'd unpacked both her bags, and it was time to retire. She heard Jesse's footsteps on the stairs and as he came down the hall. Her stomach clenched and her heart beat faster.

Jesse stopped at the door to the bedroom. "You can't put it off anymore, Clare."

She looked away from him, her gaze landing on the Chinese screen. "Put what off? I don't know what you're talking about."

"Sure you do. It's time for bed."

Butterflies dived in her stomach and she turned to Jesse. "Can't we—"

He shook his head.

"No. We can't. We're sleeping together. I'm not making love to you, but we are sleeping together. I'd like to hold you in my arms and dream of all the things I'd like to do to and with you."

Clare lifted an eyebrow. "With me?"

"You don't get to just lie there. We will make love together, maybe not the first time but as we get more familiar with each other…"

Clare stood, muscles tense. "If you say so. I've seen the animals on the farm; it seems to me that the male does everything, whether the female wants him to or not."

Jesse placed his hands on her upper arms and gazed down at her.

"Clare, we are not animals giving into the rut. We are human beings enjoying each other and the marriage bed. There is a big difference between what we will do and what animals do. Now, go on and get ready for bed."

Taking slow steps she went to the bureau and pulled her well-worn cotton nightgown out of the drawer. The gown was so old that in some places the material was nearly see through, but it was the only one she had. She hoped it didn't reveal too much. She went behind the screen to change. Taking a washcloth from the top drawer of the commode, she poured water into the basin and using the soap she found there, cleaned herself of eight days of travel grime.

Jesse laid on the bed, fully dressed except for his boots, arms behind his head, looking at her as she came from behind the Chinese silk screen.

"I'm beginning to think that screen was a bad idea."

"No, it was a wonderful idea, and I'm thankful that you bought it. I love how you furnished the house. Did you see Nora's face when she saw her room?"

Clare climbed onto the bed and lay facing him on her side, propped up by her elbow.

"She hasn't had a lot of nice things in

her life. Her home with Sol, her husband, was a one room cabin in the miner's town. A lot of those places are just one room. Some of the single men are living in tents."

"Tents! Couldn't you build a...a dormitory for the single men? They work for you, after all. You wouldn't have to provide free room, but you could charge two dollars a month for a bed or something minimal in relation to what they make. I read about factories on the East Coast that built dormitories for their workers."

Jesse raised his eyebrows and gave her a slight nod.

"That's not a bad idea. It's something all of the mine owners could go together on so no one of us would be out a lot of capital. You're a genius."

He rolled over until he was facing her, propped on one arm as she was, and kissed her. Then with the other hand he explored her. Rubbing her arm up and down, then over her hip and thigh. Light touches. He hefted one breast and rubbed her nipple through the cotton of her gown.

"Uh, Jesse, should you be doing that?" She stiffened. Was Jesse a man of his word? Would he take her anyway?

"Don't you like it? Doesn't my touch feel good?"

"Oh, yes, but you promised."

Her shallow breathing belied her pleasure and she closed her eyes feeling heat travel from her extremities to her core.

Suddenly Jesse's hand was gone and the bed shifted as he stood.

Clare's eyes flew open.

Unbuttoning his pants and then his shirt, both of them hit the floor in a pile. His under drawers soon followed, and he stood before her in his magnificence.

"Jesse! What are you doing? We are not making love."

"I know that, but you will get used to seeing my body. You're untried and I want you not to fear me. I'm just a man and my body is made to love you."

She'd seen naked men. Admittedly, it was by accident. She'd come into the kitchen too soon on bath night and seen her father as he stood drying himself from his bath.

"I can see that, but that doesn't change my mind. I want time for us to know each other better. I want my couple of days."

"And you'll have them. I don't go back

on my word, but that doesn't change my mind." He gestured up and down the length of his body. "This is how I normally sleep and you need to get used to that. You'll find it's more comfortable than sleeping with clothes on."

Clare sighed and rolled to her back. "I suppose I do need to get used to you."

He lay on the bed and lifted his arm. "Roll over here. I want to hold you."

She hesitated, stealing glances, but not moving.

"Clare, come on. I won't bite." He grinned. "Unless you want me to."

She scooted next to him and lay there stiff as a board.

"Relax."

He leaned over and kissed her cheek, then right next to her mouth on both sides, before taking her lips with his. Gentle, soft, he sipped from her in an easy motion.

She sighed and opened her mouth. Clare loved his kisses, though she didn't have anything to compare them to, she thought Jesse was the best kisser.

He didn't rush in but ran his tongue around her lips tasting her before venturing inward.

Jesse held her in place with his lips while his hands roamed unrestricted over her body. Then he suddenly quit.

"But I'm a man of my word and I won't touch you anymore until your two days are up."

"Even if I want you to?"

"Even then. You have your two days."

He kept his arm where it was.

"I'd love to hold you while you sleep, but I won't force you."

"Thank you." She scooted back to her side of the bed. She wondered just what would have happened if Jesse was not a man of his word. Would he have made love to her? Did she want him to? She certainly liked his kisses. Would she like lovemaking, too?

CHAPTER 5

She was so warm and comfortable. More so than she'd been in a long, long time. She moved her arm—oh God, she couldn't be.

"Awake now, sleepyhead?"

His voice, still gravelly from sleep, teased her.

She closed her eyes, slid her arm off his body and couldn't help but notice the flatness of his stomach and the taut muscles lying beneath the skin.

"Why didn't you wake me sooner?" Like as soon as I put my arm across your stomach.

"I was enjoying watching you sleep too much. Your little snorts among the snores."

She narrowed her gaze. "Ladies don't

snore nor do they snort."

"Well, you must not be much of a lady, since you do both."

"You are insufferable." The sun was beginning to rise, the light showing though the open curtains. She pushed herself away from him and off the bed. Then she went to the closet, pulled out a sky blue dress, and walked to the bureau for fresh under garments. She took all of the items behind the screen and dressed.

If her husband's groans meant anything, then he was severely disappointed he couldn't watch her dress. She smiled.

When she was finished she came out from behind the screen.

"Well as much as I hate that screen, you do look lovely."

Clare looked quickly at the floor and smiled. "You don't have to say those things to me. I understand."

Jesse bounded off the bed and was before her in two seconds.

"What do you understand, Clare? Tell me."

"You say nice things to me, because I'm your wife and you want to make love to me, so you have to."

Jesse took her chin gently with two of his fingers.

"I say those things because they are true. Yes, I do want to make love to you, but I would never lie in order to do so."

"You wouldn't?" She liked what he did to her the previous evening. The way he made her feel, just with his touch, was incredible.

"No, I wouldn't, that's why I stopped last night. I want you more than you can imagine, but I'll wait."

He lifted her chin and lowered his head, meeting her lips with his.

Jesse broke the kiss, but not before Clare somehow managed to wrap her arms around his neck.

"You're lovely, Clare. Anyone who ever told you different was a liar."

"Thank you."

Jesse smiled and pulled her close.

"Jesse."

"Hmm?"

"You're still naked."

"I wondered when you would notice that."

He kissed her again, deeply.

The gesture conveyed how much he

wanted her as his ready body showed her.

She broke off and stepped back. "You better get dressed. If you think you'll shock me, you won't. I grew up on a farm with three sisters and a brother and baths in the kitchen every Saturday night."

He grinned. "Afraid you'll change your mind?"

"You never know but I want my days. You tempt me and you know it, but tomorrow night or the night after, you can make love to me. Not before."

"I'll be waiting with bated breath."

"I see you've read Shakespeare."

"I like to read."

"So do I." She looked away so as not to see him in his nudity. "Come now, put on your clothes. I'll help Nora with breakfast."

He chuckled. "Be down in a few minutes."

Clare smelled the coffee when she was midway down the stairs. The heavenly aroma called to her and she hurried a little faster toward the kitchen. She practically burst through the door and headed to the cupboard for a cup. Clare couldn't pour the brew fast enough. She put the pot back on the stove and picked up her cup.

"Ahh," she breathed after her first swallow. "You make one fine cup of coffee, Nora."

"Well, thanks. Sit down and I'll start your eggs. I've got the meats done and in the oven along with the toast."

Clare heard a meow from the box. She'd moved the box far enough away from the stove that Jasper stayed warm but not too warm.

She went over and picked up the kitten and set her on the floor while she cleaned her box and then got her a saucer of milk. After she was done she retrieved the kitten from Nora, who obviously was as taken with her as Clare was, for she'd picked her up and was petting Jasper while she purred.

"There you go. Breakfast and a clean box."

Jasper lapped at the milk. Clare sat back down at the table and sipped her coffee now that her baby was taken care of.

"Nora, have you eaten?"

"No, I thought I'd wait for you and Jesse."

Clare felt guilty because she found herself so easily accepting the help Nora gave. Normally breakfast was one of the tasks she'd done at home.

"Did I hear my name?"

Jesse walked through the door, buttoning his shirt cuffs as he came.

"You did. Nora has waited to eat until we got here."

"That's mighty nice of you." He finished with his sleeve, walked to the cupboard and grabbed a cup.

"As your housekeeper, I should eat after you have done so," said Nora.

After he poured his coffee he returned to the table.

"Nonsense," said Jesse. "Besides you shouldn't wait for us anyway. If you're hungry…eat."

"I prefer to wait. After all these years of eating alone since Sol has been gone, I enjoy the company."

"How long has your husband been gone?" asked Clare.

"Four years now. Just before Jesse came to Hope's Crossing. It's been real lonely and meal times were the worst. The rest of the time you're too busy to let the loneliness in, but at meal times, when things slow down and it's just you…well, the heart break is most difficult then and at bed time. I miss having his arms around me."

Nora's eyes filled with tears, but the older woman turned away before they could fall. By the time she returned to the table with the food, the tears were gone.

Clare took the hand Jesse laid on top of the table and squeezed it. "You're a good man, Jesse Donovan."

He gave her a half smile and put his other hand on top of hers. "I hope you always think so."

She narrowed her gaze and leaned forward. "Why wouldn't I?"

"Sometimes things aren't always what they seem. Just remember I will never do anything to hurt you, if I can help it."

"That's rather cryptic."

"I'm just trying to prepare you for what might be."

"Don't you think it would be better to just tell me what's happened or may happen, so I can be prepared?"

Jesse sighed. "Yes, it is. I was trying to soften the news…well never mind. An accident occurred at the mine several months ago. Luckily no one was killed, but several of my men were injured. I found the man responsible and fired him. He's been threatening to get even with me ever since."

"What did this man do to cause the accident?" Clare took a sip of her coffee.

Jesse leaned his arms on the table and held his cup with both hands. "He came to work drunk and set off the dynamite before everyone was clear. Two of my men were grievously injured—one lost a leg, one an arm."

Clare set her cup on the table so hard the coffee sloshed out of it.

"Those men will never work in the mines again, but I won't let their families go hungry. I've hired them to work in the company store. The pay isn't as much, but at least they can provide for their families and retain their dignity."

Incensed this man should blame Jesse, Clare demanded. "Who is he?"

"His name is Harry Smith. Mostly he's just a rabble rouser, and my men don't listen to him. They know what happened. But, the newer men who weren't here then, or the men with an ax to grind...well." He shrugged.

Nora brought their plates full of fried eggs, toast, and bacon to the table.

"Harry has always been a drunk," she

said. "I sometimes wonder if he wasn't the cause of the cave-in that took my Sol from me."

Jesse nodded. "I've often wondered the same thing, but I never could prove it. Maybe if I had, Ben and Frank wouldn't be manning the company store."

"Why do you call it the company store? That's the same as the mercantile, isn't it?"

"No," said Jesse. "Smith's Mercantile is run by Lavernia for profit. The company store is not. The store also does not carry all the things the mercantile does, only the very basics. Coffee, flour, sugar, bulk items. Everyone still gets their milk, eggs, spices, and so forth from Smith's. The company store is there just to make sure families don't go hungry. Folks can get credit there when they can't at the mercantile. No one is ever turned away." Jesse took a bite of his eggs followed by one of toast.

"Sol and I had to depend on the store a few times ourselves over the years." Nora put her plate and coffee cup on the table, then sat. "My Sol wasn't a saint. He was a gambler and if I didn't get his pay before he got the urge, then we ended up at the store to make ends meet. He liked to gamble, but he wasn't very good at it."

Clare's heart went out to Nora for having to deal with a gambler for a husband. "Why not just raise the wages of the miners?"

"That's a good question, and one I'm sure a lot of the miners have themselves. The answer is hard. We pay a fair wage for a fair days work, but not all miners are good husbands and fathers. Sometimes they spend their earnings on drink, gambling and women."

"Oh. I didn't realize." Clare took a bite of her breakfast.

"We want what skills they can give us. We don't manage their lives."

"To change topics," said Clare. "Nora, breakfast is wonderful. Thank you."

"Yes," Jesse chimed in holding up a forkful of eggs and bacon. "Best I've had in a long time."

"Thank you both," said Nora. "It's kinda nice to hear someone praise my cookin' again."

"Well, I can guarantee you'll be hearing it from us. Have I told you how happy I am you're here?" Clare reached over to place her hand on Nora's arm and squeezed. "I can cook, but I don't like to. I like to bake, so I'm more than happy to make the bread, cakes, cookies, and pies while you cook and clean."

"And I'm happy I'm not having to do any of it, except for eating, of course." Jesse leaned back in his chair and patted his full stomach.

"Of course," said Nora and Clare at the same time. Then they looked at each other and laughed.

Jesse looked from one woman to the other and shook his head. Then he righted his chair and stood.

"Got to get to work."

"Where are you going?" She watched him put on his coat.

"To the mine. I have good people working for me and they generally manage just fine without me, but that doesn't mean I don't go into work every day. I'd go mad if I didn't have something to do, some work to attend to."

Clare nodded. "I know what you mean. I couldn't be a lay about either."

He bent down to Clare and gave her a kiss on the cheek. Then, gently, with his fingers moved her head until her lips were next to his and then kissed her full on the mouth right in front of Nora.

"Oh, that's lovely, just lovely." Nora got a faraway look in her eyes. "My Sol used to kiss me smack on the lips every time. He said there was no point in kissing half way."

Knowing that Nora approved didn't stop Clare from blushing. She felt warm all over and especially in her cheeks.

"Sol was a smart man," said Jesse as he turned and left the kitchen.

"Now, while you're still in the bloom of new love, let's clean up the kitchen and start your baking and my cooking."

"Yes, ma'am." Clare saluted and then broke into giggles. She loved having another woman to talk to and cook with. The situation was almost like being home and working with her mother, though Nora wasn't quite old enough. More like her older sister.

Clare and Nora baked and cleaned all day Friday. They took time out for meals and Clare had expected Jesse to come home for lunch, though she didn't know how far away the mine was from the house. When he didn't, she was a little disappointed.

He did make it home for supper.

Nora fixed a nice roasted chicken with parsley potatoes and canned green beans, and Clare baked a peach cobbler for dessert.

Jesse ate like a man starved.

"Did you eat lunch today?" Clare asked between bites. "You seem particularly hungry tonight."

"No," answered Jesse. "I was too busy to think about it. Another accident happened at the mine. One of the men was injured. Doc Kilarney says he'll make a full recovery, but it will be weeks before he can come back to work."

"Oh, my gosh, what caused the accident?" asked Nora.

"One of the roof braces snapped in half. The wood appeared like it was sawed almost all the way through."

"Who would do such a thing?" asked Clare, and then the answer hit her. "Do you think it was this Harry Smith character?"

Jesse nodded. "If not him, then someone who sympathizes with him."

"What will you do?" Nora, set her napkin on the table, her eyes wide.

"I'm hiring more guards. Currently, I have two at the entrance during the night, now I have them working during the day as well and I've warned them about Harry."

"Do they know him?" Clare asked. "Could he sneak through using another name?"

Clare got the cobbler from the counter and brought it back to the table along with the clotted cream for the top.

"Anything is possible. I can only hope I've hired the right people for this job, but I don't really know who is following him or who perhaps sympathizes with him or just who to trust."

"Surely no one wants to see their co-workers injured. Do they?" asked Clare. Her stomach knotted and she pushed her dessert away, unable to eat.

"I'm guessing they consider the injuries as collateral damage and necessary to get their point across."

"And just what is the point? That Harry Smith gets revenge and all mine owners should be hung?" asked Clare.

"Yes, and like in war, whoever else gets hurt doesn't matter. Harry wants me out of business for firing him."

"Are you going back tonight?" Apprehensive about his leaving she knew she couldn't say anything.

"Yes, just for a short while. Will you miss me?"

"Of course not." She lied, not wanting him to think she was concerned for his safety. She'd miss him a great deal. This would be her first night alone and her second night as a married woman. Was this what she had to look forward to? Lonely nights by herself? Not that she was ready to make love, she wasn't, but she did enjoy having him near.

He grinned. "Liar."

She raised her chin a notch. "Well, I never." Then she turned away and smiled.

Jesse turned her so she faced him.

"I'll miss you, too."

He lowered his head and kissed her.

"I'm glad you'll miss me. You please me, Clare. You please me very much."

Cheered by his compliment, her gaze followed him as he left the room, and a small smile eased its way across her face. Yet she couldn't help but fear for him. He was in danger. He knew it and now so did Clare.

CHAPTER 6

Jesse rode back to the mine. It would be dark before he headed home, but he wanted to observe what kind of progress the men were making and see for himself that his new guards were on duty.

His mine was the first one along the mining road. The entrance was surrounded by large boulders and bushes which he now thought should be removed. Too easy for someone to hide. If it weren't for Harry Smith, he wouldn't have worried about the vegetation.

He reined his horse to a stop in front of the mine office. Though twilight was upon him he still saw the entrance to the mine and was disturbed when he saw only one guard on duty. The other may have gone into the mine, so he tried not to let his imagination get away from him. Nonetheless he lit a lantern and pulled his Colt out of its holster before walking up to the mine.

"Hello, George. Where's Henry?" Jesse tensed and gazed around the area.

"Don't know. I had to leave for a few minutes and when I got back he was gone."

George seemed genuinely at a loss.

"Come with me and keep out your gun."

Together, he and the guard walked around the outside of the mine, checking behind bushes and boulders. They found the missing guard, unconscious behind a large group of chokecherry bushes. From the look of the head wound bleeding profusely, it appeared he'd been hit with a rock or perhaps the butt of a gun.

"George, go get your canteen. Let's get this cleaned up and see what we have here."

Jesse took his handkerchief from his pocket and dabbed at the wound. Seeing the gash through the man's hair was difficult, but he knew it would need stitches.

Henry's eyelids flickered and he started coming around.

Where was George with that canteen?

"Henry. Henry, can you hear me?"

"Ow." He reached up and touched his head. "What'd ya want to go an' do that for, George?"

"Henry." Jesse shook the man's shoulders a little. "Pay attention. Did George do this to you?"

"Boss? That you? What you doin' here?"

"I came up to check on the mine. Looks like it's a good thing I did, too."

"George hit me. Why'd he go and do that for?"

"I don't know Henry, but I can guess."

In the distance, Jesse heard the pounding of a horse galloping away from the mine. George.

"Can you get up? We need to get you to the doctor."

"Who's gonna watch the mine?"

Jesse sighed and glanced around. "No one, which is the way Harry Smith wanted it. But, there's nothing to be done for it. Can you ride? Do I need to get the buckboard?"

"Naw, Boss, I kin ride if you got a horse."

Henry stood.

But the man swayed enough so that Jesse had to catch him before he fell over.

"I'll help you. Let's go."

Jesse put Henry's arm over his shoulder and guided the man down the mountain path. There he helped him onto Jesse's own horse and then mounted behind him. Together they rode to Hope's Crossing and Dr. Kilarney.

"Doc." Jesse knocked hard on the door to the doctor's office. Dr. Kilarney lived in the back part of a house that housed both his living quarters and clinic.

"Hold your horses, I'm coming."

The door opened and the doctor greeted him with an irritated gaze.

"What happened?"

The doctor came out and helped Jesse get Henry inside.

"He's one of the guards of my mine. The other guard cold-cocked him. He's been bleeding a lot since I found him."

Doc scoffed. "Head wounds always bleed a lot."

The doctor assisted them down a hall into a room. A tall, skinny table was situated in the center of the stark room with its white washed walls and wooden floor. No pictures, nothing except bare walls.

Henry was weak and unable to give them much assistance.

"Let's get him onto the table," said Doc.

"I'm sorry," Henry said. "I don't seem to have any strength."

"He may have a concussion. I'm keeping him overnight. I've got a spare bedroom for just such circumstances."

"If you've got this, Doc, I need to get back to the mine. I've got to find out what Harry Smith is planning."

"Go. Make people safe. I don't want to have to come to the mine and treat any injuries, including yours, so be careful."

Jesse patted the doctor on the back. "Always, Doc. Always. Especially now that I'm a married man." He imagined Clare's dark red hair spread out on the pillow. "I don't want to make Clare a widow just yet."

Doc Kilarney raised an eyebrow. "I should hope not. She'd be inundated with male callers. Not only because she'd suddenly be a single woman, but a single, rich woman."

Jesse nodded. "I know and I don't intend for her to be single again. Ever."

"Good man."

"Thanks, Doc. I'll check back on Henry later."

"He's fine. Go make sure that mine is safe."

Jesse didn't need to be told again. The longer he was away, the more time that Harry Smith or his cohorts had to sabotage the mine.

He rode his black gelding, Jericho, as hard and fast as he safely could.

When he reached the property he rode clear to the mine entrance rather than stop at his office and leave the horse. He needed all the time he could get to find and hopefully stop anything they might have planned.

The lantern he'd left there earlier was still on the ground outside the entry. He lit it and then held the light aloft while he entered the mine. He was about half way down the shaft when he saw them. His stomach churned and his heart beat faster at the sight of six sticks of dynamite, three on each of the two of the main support beams. Luckily, whoever set them up didn't know that much about dynamite. Jesse went to the supports and pulled the fuses out of each stick, thereby rendering them safe.

He followed the fuse wire back to the

plunger. No one was there. There was no need to be since no one was working now. Thank goodness he quit running the second shift. He left the fuse where it was to make it look like no one had found it. Tomorrow he'd be waiting for whoever came to use the plunger, with Sam Longworth along to arrest the person. He just hoped it was Harry Smith who decided to blow the mine up in person, but he didn't believe he'd get that lucky.

He went back to Jericho mounted and rode home. Clare would be waiting. He longed to sink into her warmth but he'd settle for her safely in his arms. She'd only been there for two full days and one night and he was already possessive of her. That was all right. She was his wife and he wouldn't let anything happen to her.

When Jesse arrived home there was light emanating from the kitchen. Clare. He felt warm inside that someone would care enough about him to wait up for him to return home.

He took care of Jericho, got him settled into his stall, brushed and combed, fed with hay, oats and water. Then Jesse headed to the house.

Opening the door to the kitchen, he was glad he wasn't mistaken.

Clare sat at the table, holding Jasper. As soon as he opened the door she set the kitten down, ran to him and launched herself into his arms.

"I've been so worried. You were gone so long. Are you all right?"

She started running her hands over him, searching for wounds.

"I'm fine. Come now, get me a cup of coffee, and I'll tell you all about my evening."

"You can tell me in bed, while you hold me in your arms."

Jesse smiled. "Not changing your mind and letting me make love to you, huh?"

"I wasn't that worried," she retorted. But she smiled, too.

"As much as I enjoy you being in my arms, I know you must be tired. Me? I'm just the opposite. I need to wind down before I'll be able to go to sleep. You go on ahead."

"Come with me, I'll help you."

She held her hand out to him.

He decided to forgo the coffee and took her outstretched hand. She led him upstairs to their bedroom.

"Take off your shirt and lay on your stomach."

He did as she asked.

Clare sat next to him on the bed.

Then he felt her hands on his back rubbing his shoulders and kneading the muscles underneath.

"That feels wonderful."

He felt his muscles relax under her kind ministrations

"My mother used to do this for my father after he'd had a particularly grueling day. He said he always felt better, was able to relax and get a good night's sleep."

Clare kept rubbing, up and down his back, over his shoulders and then down his arms.

"There. How do you feel now?"

"Much better." He sat up next to her on the bed. "Thank you, Clare. That was very kind of you."

"You're welcome." She sat with her hands in her lap, stealing glances at his bare chest. Her father had never looked like Jesse. Jesse was all muscle. "We should always strive to be kind to each other. We are married after all and I hope that beyond that, we'll become friends as well."

Jesse thought about what she said and what she'd done. She'd given of herself to him, not in that she let him make love to her and yet with her hands she'd made love to him. "I'd like that, to be friends as well as lovers."

She ducked her head and blushed.

He reached over and tucked an errant curl behind her ear. "You look so pretty when you blush. The pink rises up your neck and stops at your cheeks, giving you a lovely color. Some women use cosmetics to achieve that shade. They've usually long passed the bloom of youth."

"I don't use cosmetics."

"I know and I'm glad. I want to know that you're always being honest with me even when you blush."

Clare shook her head. "You're a strange man, Jesse Donovan. A very strange man."

"Get your clothes off and prepare for bed. I'm ready to feel you in my arms, your body next to mine."

He rose from the bed and removed the remainder of his clothes, then got between the sheets and waited.

Clare went behind the screen and hung

her dress over the top of it before she removed the rest of her clothes. Then she washed herself before putting on her nightgown and coming from behind the screen.

"You'll have to get used to sleeping without that."

He waved his hand up and down in front of her.

"That may be, but not tonight."

She climbed in on her side of the bed, blew out the lamp and lay on her back.

"Are you trying to avoid me?"

"No. Who said I was avoiding you? Am I not the one who suggested you tell me what happened tonight, while you held me in your arms?"

"Yes, you did. You were in my arms just this morning as a matter of fact."

"That's only because I was cold and you were so warm and…"

"And?"

She huffed. "Comfortable. It should not be comfortable for me to sleep with you."

"You're married to me now. You should be comfortable sleeping with me."

She shook her head. "No, not so soon. That's not normal."

Jesse laughed. "Normal doesn't exactly describe us. You're a mail-order bride remember?"

"Yes, I remember." She let out a sigh. "A replacement for the fiancée who changed her mind about marrying you. A replacement bride."

Jesse got quiet…remembering Rebecca's letter. The pain had been greater than he'd ever let on to anyone. "That's right."

"I'll never forget I'm your replacement bride. I wish I could just be a bride in my own right?"

He moved back to his side of the bed and put his arm behind his head.

"I hadn't realized that I'd done anything to keep you from being a bride or anything else you wanted to. You only arrived yesterday."

"I know." She turned to face him, propping herself on one arm as she had the night before. "But when you introduce me I don't want to be introduced as your replacement bride."

He was confused. "I haven't done that yet, why would I start now? You're my wife and that's how I'll introduce you as my wife, Clare Donovan."

"Thank you. I'm sorry. I've let my imagination run rampant. I shouldn't have."

"I don't understand why you're so worried about being my replacement bride. Except for when I first told you I haven't mentioned it again. Have I?"

The light of the full moon glowed in their room and he saw her bite the inside of her lip.

"No. No, you haven't. My own worries and imagination are rearing their ugly head."

He suddenly realized that he'd hurt her feelings when he called her his replacement bride. He stretched his arm out onto her pillow.

"Come here."

She hesitated for a moment and then scooted next to him, letting his arms enclose her.

This was right. He hadn't known what he was missing until now. He'd been missing her, a wife.

"One of the guards I hired knocked out the other man working with him. Either he planted the dynamite in the mine, or he let in someone who did. Six sticks were set to blow probably after my men were already down the shaft, trapping and more than likely killing them."

"Oh, my God." Clare's hand flew to her throat. "Why would anyone want to do that? They must be insane. Do you think it's this Harry Smith fellow?"

"I do. But again, I have nothing to prove it. I took the fuses out of the dynamite so it's harmless, but I didn't remove the sticks. I didn't think about it until now. I must go first thing in the morning and take those sticks out of there before someone finds them."

"But, I thought you said you rendered them harmless."

"I did. For now. There's nothing stopping someone from putting fuses back in them and using them again."

"Oh, no."

"Yes. It was dumb of me but I'll get there before the shift starts and it will be fine. Nothing to worry about."

He felt her nervous quiver against him. If he was to admit it himself, it could be a dangerous situation and he would need his wits about him.

So he waited. He needed to rest, but even with Clare comfortingly in his arms, he couldn't slow his mind. Every time he closed his eyes he saw the shaft blow up with his men inside. He dug frantically to get them out, his hands bleeding from moving the rocks and dirt.

Each time the end was the same. He saw bodies scattered across the tunnel floor. Every time he woke in a cold sweat.

Finally, he rose from the bed careful to let Clare sleep. Then he dressed and went down-stairs. In the kitchen he scratched out a note to Clare, setting it on the table before he left the house.

CHAPTER 7

Clare awoke alone. Jesse was nowhere in sight and his side of the bed was cold. He'd been gone for a while.

She threw back the blankets, got out of bed, and dressed, before hurrying downstairs.

When she reached the kitchen, Nora was sitting at the table with a cup of coffee.

"Where is he?" Her heart was in her throat, beating much too fast.

"Calm down." Nora waved her over to the table. "He said you'd be upset. You've only been married a couple of days. How can you know he'd be doing something dangerous this morning?"

"He went to the mine without waking

me, didn't he?"

"Yes. He left you this note."

Nora handed her the piece of paper.

She read the scribbling on the sheet.

Clare,

I know you will worry, but I didn't want to wake you. I've gone to get the dynamite before anyone else can make use of it. I'll see you at breakfast time.

Jesse

"What time is it? When is breakfast time? We've not been married long enough for me to know."

Nora reached out a hand and touched Clare's arm. "Calm down, Clare. It's still early. We'll go on and make breakfast. Before you know it he'll be home. Why don't you go do Jesse's chores? I know he's got at least one cow to milk and eggs to gather."

Clare closed her eyes and took a deep breath. "Of course, you're right. I'm letting my imagination get the better of me again. It's a weakness of mine."

"We all do it." Nora assured her.

"I'll be right back."

She went out to the barn, found the milking stool and an empty milk bucket.

Clare patted the back of the cow to let her know she wasn't alone. She didn't even know if the cow had a name—for now she'd call her Flossy.

"Hello there, Flossy. I'm sitting right here and getting that milk out of you before you end up in pain. It's a good thing I was raised on a farm and know how to do this. Actually this was one of my favorite chores. I'd go out and talk to the cows while I milked them. It was better than having a diary."

Clare sat the stool next to the cow, close enough that she could reach the udder. Then she squeezed off a few squirts for the barn cats, got a couple of them in the face, and laughed, and then filled the pail. When Flossy had given all she could give, Clare stood, picked up the stool and went to the next cow. This one she called Bessie. When she was done with her, she put the milking stool back against the wall where she'd found it and took the buckets full of milk into the house.

Clare set the containers on the counter and looked at Nora.

The other woman shook her head.

Jesse wasn't back yet.

Clare picked up the egg basket and went out to the chicken coop. Gathering eggs was not one of her favorite chores. She invariably got pecked by at least one hen, when she tried to take the hen's egg.

The bin with the grain for the birds was on the side of the coop. She scooped a container full of corn into her apron. From there she spread it by handfuls across the chicken yard. When she'd finished with that, she entered the coop itself and gathered the eggs. For the nests where the chickens were gone, it was easy to scoop up the egg and put it in the basket. If the hen was still sitting on the nest then Clare had to lift the bird with one hand and grab the egg with the other, all the while hoping the fowl didn't have time to peck her.

By the time she had gathered all fourteen eggs, she'd managed to only get pecked once. All in all that wasn't too bad for her first time with these chickens. As she did the chore more often and got used to these hens, she'd get in and out without a scratch. She took the basket back to the house, hoping Jesse had returned and not taken his horse to the barn.

She walked into the kitchen and looked

expectantly at Nora.

"Before you say anything, he hasn't come back yet," said Nora. She had a bucket of milk in her hands and was pouring the contents through cheesecloth into a milk can.

Clare poured a cup of coffee and sat at the table. No sooner had she sat than she was up again. "I guess I can wash those eggs so we can get them put away."

She filled a pan with water from the pump at the sink and set it on the stove to heat. When the liquid was hot she poured part of it into a basin with soap chips and left the rest in the pan to which she added more cold water until it was just cool. Clare took the eggs one at a time and washed all the dirt, straw and feces off, getting them ready to use or sell.

When she was done, she checked the clock on the counter and saw that only fifteen minutes had passed. The time was now eight o'clock and no Jesse. The knots in her stomach grew tighter.

Nora grasped Clare's elbow and guided her to the table. "Come on now, you keep checking that clock and you'll make yourself crazy. Sit, drink your coffee, eat breakfast with me and then we'll start our work for the day. There could be a million reasons why he hasn't come home yet."

Clare stopped and looked at Nora, her body tense. "Or there could be just one. Would we hear the explosion from here if the mine blew up?"

"Probably not. The mine's west of town a couple of miles."

"Well, we have that dinner party tonight, so I guess I better get busy. If I don't, I'll go crazy. I'm supposed to be a bride not a widow. "

"And I've no intention of making you a widow any time soon."

Jesse walked through the kitchen door.

Clare's gaze flew to him. She didn't think she'd seen anything more wonderful.

"Jesse." She wanted to run into his arms, but she remained in place, letting her gaze take him in. His sleeve was torn and blood ran down his hand. She gasped. "You're hurt. What happened?"

She went to him and led him to the table, making him sit.

"It's nothing."

"It's not nothing, you're bleeding all over my, I mean Nora's, nice clean floor.

Now what happened? Did you run into Harry Smith? Is the man in jail now?"

"No. The culprit wasn't Harry. George was back and he'd seen that I'd taken out the fuses and was replacing them. We had a scuffle and I got wounded. It's just a scratch."

"Take off your shirt."

"You'll have to help me with that."

Clare lifted an eyebrow but unbuttoned his shirt and removed the garment from the uninjured arm first. She started to do the same to the injured arm, but Jesse flinched.

"This is more than a scratch."

"Yeah, George had a knife and was able to use it before…"

A knife? Her stomach clenched. "Before what?"

"Before I killed him."

Clare gasped. "Oh, no, Jesse, I'm so sorry." She couldn't imagine having to kill a man.

She carefully removed the shirt sleeve from his arm and then saw the wounds.

"My God, Jesse." She was prepared for the four-inch long gash along his arm but not the hole in his side half that long. "You'll need stitches and that stab wound needs to be cauterized." Just like Pa's wound did when he sliced open his leg with the scythe. "I can do it, I've seen it done, but we'd be better off having the doctor look at it."

"No!" his free hand grabbed her forearm. "I don't want Harry Smith to know I'm wounded. You do it."

"All right. I need to clean the wounds. It'll hurt, but I'll be as gentle as I can. Do you have a bottle of whiskey?"

Jesse shook his head. "You are not putting that stuff on me. Just wash them with the lye soap and then stitch it up."

Clare nodded. "As you wish. Nora, would you hand me a towel, please?"

Nora went to the drawer of dish towels.

"Hold that," her chin jutted toward the cloth in Nora's hand, "on your side while I stitch up your arm."

Nora handed Jesse the towel.

"I have to heat a knife to seal your side." Clare went to the knife drawer and selected a good-sized one with a very flat blade. "I can try just stitching the hole shut but sealing it with the heat would be better."

Jesse tried to take a deep breath. But Clare saw that the movement hurt him.

"Do what you have to."

She put the knife on the stove under a cast iron skillet so the blade would heat on both sides.

Thirty minutes later, she'd stitched the slice in his arm closed, wrapped the bicep in white bandages, and was ready to cauterize the stabbing site. Pa and her brother were always injuring themselves to some extent or another on the farm. She hadn't had to do this kind of thing for a while and thought she was leaving repairing wounds behind her.

"Okay, let me get the knife." She got a towel to pick up the hot knife. "When I say to, pull away your towel." She positioned the knife above the wound. "All right. Now."

As soon as he pulled the cloth out of the way, Clare laid the flat of the hot knife blade against Jesse's side and pressed.

"Dear God!" His whole body went rigid and Jesse hollered.

Clare had to bite her lip to keep from yelling herself. She hated causing him pain. After a few seconds Clare pulled the knife blade away and examined the site of the bleeding.

The horrible stench of burnt flesh filled the air.

"It's stopped. The bleeding has stopped."

"Thank God. I couldn't go through that again."

"I'm sorry I had to hurt you. Let me get you bandaged. I want to change these every day and keep a good eye on both wounds to make sure neither site becomes infected. If they do—"

"They won't," replied Jesse as forcefully as he could. He looked toward the stove. "As long as it's still morning, how about some breakfast?"

She raised her eyebrows. "You're hungry?"

"Yeah, I could eat."

She shook her head in disbelief. "What would you like?"

"Just eggs and toast. Then I think I'll go back to bed. For some reason I feel a little weak."

"All right. I'll get you a cup of coffee and then start on your breakfast."

"I got breakfast, you get him the coffee," said Nora, who had remained quiet through Jesse's ordeal. "And then scrub the table before I set down his plate."

Clare nodded and busied herself getting the drink. Her hands shook and she sloshed coffee onto the counter. She cursed under her breath and steadied the cup with her other hand while she walked to the table with it. Then while Jesse sipped on the coffee she scrubbed the table in front of him clean of any blood.

"Now tell me how George did this and should I go get Sam and let him know?"

"I stopped at Sam and Jo's on the way home. I didn't put Jericho away though, if you wouldn't mind…"

"No, of course not. I'll see to that now. Then, after you eat I'll help you into bed and you can tell me what happened."

Clare walked out the front door and saw Jericho standing by the hitching rail. He wasn't tied to the rail, just standing before it as though he was tied there. The reins hung loose from the bridle to the ground.

She approached the horse, picked up the reins and led him back to the barn. Once there she lit the lantern that was affixed to the wall and then put Jericho in his stall, removed the bridle, saddle bags and the saddle. There was blood on the saddle, but she'd scrub it after she was done with Jericho. She rubbed him down with clean, dry straw, curried and brushed him. Then she gave him a flake of hay and measure of oats in his trough, which was half of a barrel nailed to the stall wall.

The tack room was in the back of the barn. From there she got a rag and soap and water which she used to remove the blood from the saddle before the stain had completely settled into the leather. Then she rubbed linseed oil into the leather.

After she'd thoroughly cleaned the leather, she laid the saddle and saddle bags over the saw horse, there for that purpose, then she went back up to the house. Jesse had finished his breakfast and was drinking a cup of coffee, a forearm braced on the tabletop.

"Are you ready to go to bed?" she asked.

"Yeah. More than ready."

He stood, swayed, and righted himself with the help of the table.

"Jesse! Let me help you."

Clare wrapped her arm around his waist.

"Put your arm around me."

"This isn't exactly what I had in mind when I said I wanted you in my arms."

"Now is not the time for jests. You need to get in bed and rest." She guided him to the foot of the stairs.

"Why don't you lay with me and I'll tell you what happened."

"All right, but first, do you have any laudanum or willow bark tea?"

"A small bottle of laudanum is in the pantry near to where you got these bandages."

She opened the bedroom door. "Let me help you out of your clothes and into bed." She pulled back the blankets and put both pillows on his side of the bed.

"Aren't you afraid you might see something?"

He tried to grin, but grimaced instead.

"I'm not afraid. I've seen your parts before. I was raised in the country. I've helped deliver babies, heal the sick and care for the injured. It's part of what I learned to do, part of what was expected of me as someone's wife."

"In other words, you won't be surprised by anything you see."

"That's right. Besides I've seen you naked. You've flaunted yourself before me for the last two nights. Now sit down and I'll take off your boots"

She pulled off his footwear, unbuckled his belt and unbuttoned his pants. Then she removed his pants expecting to see under drawers. Jesse wasn't wearing any. Instead she saw his manhood, his rather large manhood.

"Oh, my."

"Thought you couldn't be surprised."

He winked at her.

"I was greatly mistaken. Up close it seems...bigger. " She felt the heat rise in her and settle in two points her cheeks, and her woman's core. Good grief, what had she taken on marrying this man?

"Don't be scared. Looks like it'll be some time before I can make love to you."

"Let's not even think about that now. Just lie back while I'll get the laudanum. The drug will help you sleep, and that's what you need more than anything."

"I'm holding you to your promise you'd lay down with me."

"I haven't forgotten. I'll bring some pillows from the spare rooms. You should be propped up with that side injury."

He lay back on the pillows and let out a sigh. Clare lifted his legs and put them under the blankets, then pulled the covers up under his arms.

"I'll be right back with the medicine and fresh water."

She grabbed the pitcher off the bureau and hurried from the room.

In the kitchen, she checked the pantry and found the bottle of laudanum. It was nearly full, but that was to be expected since the dosage was no more than five drops at a time.

Clare put the little bottle in her apron pocket, filled the pitcher from the pump at the sink and grabbed a clean glass from the cupboard before rushing back upstairs to Jesse.

He laid there with his eyes closed and she wondered if he'd fallen asleep, but he opened them as soon as she entered the room.

"I thought maybe you wouldn't need the medicine to sleep."

"Closing my eyes makes the pain easier to tolerate."

Clare set the pitcher and the glass on the bureau, took the bottle of laudanum from her pocket and fixed Jesse a glass with the full dose. Without a doctor she was afraid to give him any more than that.

She went to the bed. "Here now, drink this all down."

"Then you'll lie with me?"

"While you tell me what happened."

"Very well. At least until I pass out."

She nodded. "Or until you pass out."

Clare knew from having had to take the medicine herself that is was nasty.

Jesse drank the vile stuff and then lay back as though it had taken all his energy to sit up enough to drink.

Clare took the glass, refilled it with fresh water and set it on the nightstand within his reach. Luck had been with Jesse when he was wounded, as the injuries were on his left side and he slept on the right side of the bed, nearest the door. He'd be able to reach the water if he needed it from his nightstand and they wouldn't have to switch sides of the bed.

She went around to her side and lay down beside him. Close, but far enough away that she didn't touch him.

As soon as she was settled she heard him begin to talk.

"I went back to the mine, sure I was there early enough to get the dynamite and leave."

Jesse stopped and breathed for a moment before continuing.

He was growing weak. Clare worried that he'd lost too much blood. Once he fell asleep, she thought she'd make a beef broth to rebuild his blood.

"George was there. We scuffled for the dynamite, and I knocked him to the ground. Whilst he was down I pulled the sticks from the wooden brace. George lunged at me with his knife and slashed my arm. I attempted to block his next blow but wasn't completely successful, hence the wound in my side."

He tried to laugh but winced instead.

Fear clogged her throat. "Oh, Jesse, you could have been killed."

"I managed to push him off and he fell back. When I saw him stand and raise the knife again, I pulled my Colt and shot him. He stumbled but kept coming and I shot him again. He finally fell to the dirt. Did you bring in the saddle bags?"

"No. Should I have?"

"The dynamite is in them. I'd feel better if it was in the house and not in the barn where anyone can get to it."

"Since you told me it's safe without the

fuses, I'll go get it as soon as I go back downstairs otherwise it would be staying in the barn."

"You're staying until I go to sleep?"

"I want you to just relax and let the medicine do its work. Close your eyes and just breathe."

"You won't have to stay long, I'm feeling fairly sleepy as it is."

"I don't mind. I've no place else I'd rather be."

"You're a good wife, Clare Donovan."

"And you're a good husband, Jesse Donovan, when you're not trying to get yourself killed."

Jesse didn't answer.

Clare glanced over at him.

His eyes were closed, his breathing even. He slept.

She eased herself off the bed, hurried down the stairs and out to the barn. When she reached the building she saw that the door was unlatched and stilled. She was sure she'd closed and latched it when she'd left before. Clare looked around for something she could use as a weapon and saw a pitchfork that hadn't been put away properly.

Carefully, she opened the door, propped it open for extra light and went inside, holding the pitchfork before her. She lit the lantern on the wall but still didn't see anyone. Walking carefully, continuously looking around her, she went to the saw horse holding the saddle and saddle bags.

She sucked in a breath. The saddle was there but the bags were gone.

CHAPTER 8

Clare ran back to the house. Her heart racing, she had to tell Jesse. Then she realized that he was sleeping and must have his rest. Nothing could be done about the explosives now anyway. She could go and tell Sam. At least then someone would be aware of the situation.

"Nora, I need to run an errand. I'll be back in a bit. Would you listen for Jesse and if he wakens tell him I'll return shortly."

Nora looked up from washing the dishes and nodded. "Sure. You sound like you're worried about something."

Worried! Good grief what have I gotten myself into by marrying this man? "You may as well know as the situation could involve all of us, but Jesse brought home dynamite from the mine in his saddle bags. When I went to get the bags just now I discovered they were gone." She looked down and loosened her white knuckled grip on the back of the kitchen chair. "Jesse was followed from the mine, that's the only explanation."

Nora dried her hands on the dish towel. Clare saw they were shaking. "Probably Harry or one of his men."

"That's what I figure as well. I don't want to concern Jesse with something he can't do anything about anyway, so I'm telling Sam. As sheriff, he'll want to know someone's stolen the explosives."

Clare wrapped her flowered shawl around her shoulders.

"I remember where the jail is and it's not a far walk. I'll be back within the hour."

"Hopefully, Jesse won't wake up and want to know where you are."

"If he does, just tell him I'm indisposed and have him take some more of the laudanum. Maybe while I'm out I'll go to the mercantile and pick up a bit of willow bark tea. That will help him when he's healed enough not to need the strong medicine any longer."

Nora nodded.

"You best hurry and get back here. I don't think he'll believe me that you're indisposed for any length of time. He saw how worried you were, just as I did."

Clare closed her eyes and nodded. "I'll hurry."

*****

Clare walked then ran for a bit and then walked again, so she could get to the sheriff's office as fast as possible. She passed small houses, with neat little flower gardens out front.

No businesses stood between her home and the jail which was too bad. She wouldn't be able to stop, but she could have looked while walking by. Maybe then she could concentrate on something besides Jesse lying helpless in bed.

When she reached the jail, she stopped and caught her breath before entering. Clare rapped on the door and then opened it.

"Sheriff? Sam?"

No one answered. She checked the pin watch on her bodice. Lunch time wouldn't be for another couple of hours. Clare left and walked next door to Sam and Jo's home.

She knocked on the door. After a few moments Jo answered, holding her baby.

"Good morning, can I help you?"

"Good morning. I'm Clare Donovan, Jesse's wife, and I need to talk to the sheriff right away."

"He's not here. Did you check the jail?" Jo shook her head. "What am I thinking? Of course you did. Please come in. Let's sit." She waved toward the blue damask sofa.

"No thanks." She wrung her reticule in her hands, realized what she was doing and stopped. "I can't stay. Jesse's been wounded and I don't want to leave him for long."

"Wounded? You really should come in and tell me everything. I'll make sure Sam knows. I used to be a bounty hunter myself, so have some history with law enforcement. Sit. Please."

"Only if I can hold, your little one. I hope Jesse and I are blessed with children."

"Certainly, this is Paul. He was named after his grandfather, who is the blacksmith here in town."

"That's so nice. Anyway…" Clare told Jo the whole story, as Jesse had told her and then about the dynamite being stolen. "I thought Sam should know in case he runs across the explosives anywhere or in case someone uses them."

"I'll let him know," she reached over and set her hand on Clare's knee. "Don't worry about that. You can go home now and take care of your husband. Weren't we were supposed to be at your house for dinner tonight. That's not happening now. Would you like me to let everyone else know?"

"That would be wonderful. In addition to you and Sam, there were the nine other mine owners and their wives." Clare rattled off the names she'd memorized, then kissed baby, Paul, on his head and handed him back to his mother.

"I appreciate all your help. I have to go to the mercantile and pick up a package of willow bark tea."

"Oh, it's not a problem at all and I've got some white willow bark tea you can have." Jo stood.

Clare followed suit.

"It will save you a trip to the store and get you home sooner."

"Thank you, so much. I would like to get back to him quickly."

"Come with me."

The two women walked back to the

kitchen where Jo got the tea from the pantry.

"Here you are. When Jesse gets better and you can get out, you can pay me back."

Tears filled Clare's eyes. This gesture was about the nicest thing anyone had ever done for her. She'd always been the one to share, rarely the other way around.

"Thank you. I should get back."

Jo pointed the toward Clare's house. "Save yourself some time and cut across the back yard between the house and the barn."

Clare hugged Jo lightly, since she was holding Paul and Clare didn't want to squish the baby. She left through the kitchen door.

Once outside, she ran toward their barn and then made a right to the street and then walked quickly the rest of the way home.

When Clare entered the kitchen, Nora stood at the stove stirring something in a large pot.

"Did he wake up while I was gone?"

"Nope. Haven't heard a peep out of him."

"Good. Jo loaned me the willow bark tea that I needed and saved me a trip to the mercantile. I'll put it in the pantry on the shelf with the bandages and where the laudanum goes. Jo also said she would contact everyone to cancel the dinner for tonight. We'll try again when Jesse is better. What are you cooking?"

"Beef broth. I guessed you'd be making some for him, I thought I'd get it started for you."

"Thank you. Your soup is probably better than mine anyway. I told you I'm not much of a cook. We have to cook that roast and the ham. They'll spoil before the next dinner party."

"I'll start that roast as soon as I finish this soup. And I bet your cooking is just fine. You just never had anyone tell you so. Your ma did the cooking at home I expect."

"Yes, Daddy always liked her meals best. But I always did the baking. My bread and rolls were always light and tasty." Clare laughed. "Mother's were like bricks."

"Clare."

She barely heard him. Jesse was awake but his voice sounded weak.

"I'm coming," she called. Then she looked back to Nora. "Would you put some water on for tea? That will be better for him than coffee."

"Sure thing."

Nora picked up the tea kettle and went to

the sink.

Clare rushed up the stairs to her bedroom. There she found Jesse sitting on the side of the bed. Gasping, she hurried to him.

"What are you doing up?"

"I needed to." He jutted his chin toward the Chinese screen with the chamber pot behind it.

"Do you need my help getting back into bed?"

"No, I just need to rest a minute."

"You're weak as a newborn kitten. Let me help you."

"Speaking of kittens…" He cocked his eyebrow and looked over at her pillow. Jasper had made himself quite comfortable and was happily napping.

"He wants to make sure you're all right. I told you he loves you."

"Hmpft. Dang cat will probably start purring and wake me up."

Clare laughed at his grumpiness. "He probably will."

Jesse's color was getting better. She looked down and saw his bandages were still clean. No seepage.

Clare went to the bed and held an arm

around his shoulders while he reclined back onto the pillows and then covered him with the blankets.

"How are you feeling other than weak?"

She tucked the covers along his right side.

"I've definitely felt better."

"I should hope so. Nora's got broth simmering. As soon as it's ready I'll bring you a cup. That will help you to get strong again. You should also know that I went to talk to Sam."

"Why?"

Clare wrung her hands. "The saddle bags are gone. Someone stole them from the barn."

Jesse's brows furrowed. "In that little bit of time between when you cared for Jericho and went back to get them, they were stolen?"

"Yes. Someone must have followed you from the mine. What if they had killed you?"

"They didn't. Killing me would have brought the law down on them. They want to do more damage than just kill me."

She sat on the edge of the bed next to him.

"What will we do? We can't just wait for someone to make another attempt or for this Harry Smith person to get lucky and blow up the mine next time. That would possibly kill someone and for sure put all your employees out of work."

"This is just what he wants. He wants to ruin me. Did you see anyone when you went back to the barn?"

Clare watched Jesse. He was worn out. This conversation was taking what strength he had.

"No one. Nothing we can do about it for now. Sam will probably want to talk to you after he gets home tonight, and Jo tells him everything. That being the case, you should take some more of the laudanum and get rest so you have your strength back up when he comes by. Oh, and I cancelled the dinner party. Jo is contacting everyone for me, since I don't know them. We'll try again in a couple of weeks."

Jesse nodded.

"I suppose you're right about the party and Sam. Though I don't know what I can tell him that you didn't tell Jo."

"You never know, something might occur to you when you talk to him that hasn't up until then."

She prepared the medicine in a half glass of water.

Jesse drank it all down without stopping.

Clare poured him a fresh glass of water and he drank half of it.

"Thirsty?"

He shook his head. "Trying to get the nasty taste out of my mouth."

"Ah," she nodded.

"Will you lie with me again?"

"If you like."

He winced when he moved but eased over until he was in the middle of the bed nonetheless.

"Now, I can hold you in my arms."

Jesse raised his uninjured right arm and waved it at her.

She smiled, shooed Jasper off the pillow and moved them so he was elevated and lay down beside him, cuddling to his side.

Jasper walked up Jesse's leg and made himself comfortable on his thigh.

Jesse shook his head, smiled at the kitten and hugged Clare close with his good arm.

"Now this is more what I had in mind, minus Jasper."

Clare admitted lying next to him with

his arm around her was very nice. Comfortable even, though she still wasn't use to it. She felt herself relax into his body.

"That's better. Relax. I won't bite. Unless—"

"I want you to. I remember."

She heard the smile in his voice and looked up into his brown eyes, now twinkling with either merriment or fever. Clare wasn't sure which. "You're a scoundrel, Mr. Donovan."

"Only with you, Mrs. Donovan." He bent his neck and took her lips with his. The kiss was sweet. Though she wanted more than sweet, she was grateful he felt well enough to kiss her at all. He broke away, kissed her forehead and then lay back.

"You're worn out, Jesse. Don't think of anything but me holding you." She moved her arm from her side to lie across his stomach, well away from his injury.

"I am tired."

"The medicine is taking effect. Don't fight it."

"Wake me when Sam comes, if I'm not already awake."

"I will, I promise." She wanted to reassure him that he wouldn't be left out. "I imagine he'll bring Jo and Paul with him. That baby is so adorable."

"Like one of our own someday?"

"Oh yes. Most definitely."

He squeezed her shoulders. "You know how that happens don't you?"

Clare laid her head on his chest and smiled. "Yes, I'm well aware how babies are begot."

"When I'm well, I intend to make love to you all night long. But I definitely need my strength for that."

She thought about making love to him. Was she ready? Would she ever be? Maybe by the time he was well, she wouldn't be scared any more. He did say he would take care of her. "There you go again, being a rascal."

"No, I'm being honest. When I'm healed we are getting to know each other very well. Now why don't you see about that beef broth? I feel like I could eat something."

"Are you sure? You'll be asleep within the next ten minutes or so."

"I want to start building my strength." He stopped, his words slower. "Maybe just half a cup?"

She scooted to the side of the bed and

stood. "All right. I'll be right back. Do you want me to take Jasper with me?" She nodded toward the kitten.

He looked over at the baby cat next to him. "No. He's comfortable."

When she got to the kitchen, Clare ladled some of the hot broth into a cup and carried it back upstairs. She looked to the bed as she entered and saw that Jesse was already asleep. She wasn't surprised. Clare turned around and went back down-stairs. As she reached the bottom, a knock sounded on the door.

"I've got it, Nora," she said to the woman coming up the hall toward her.

Clare pulled open the door. Sheriff Sam Longworth and his family were on her porch.

"Sam, Jo. Come in. Come in. I didn't expect you until this evening. Jesse just went back to sleep."

She stood back and let them pass into the house.

"I thought we should come as soon as possible after Jo told me about your visit. But, we're here to make sure Jesse's all right." said Sam.

"Let's go into the parlor. Nora, please

get us some coffee."

"Comin' right up."

Nora hurried back to the kitchen.

"Make yourselves comfortable. I have to go and get Jesse. He wants to be present to talk to you."

"Is he well enough," asked Sam.

"If you ask me, no. But if you ask him—"

"Yes."

Jesse stood in the doorway wearing just his pants.

"I hope you don't mind my attire. I couldn't get my shirt on by myself."

"We don't care what you wear," said Jo. "We're just glad you can get out of bed."

"I'll get you a shirt." Clare hurried from the room.

"Where shall we start?" asked Sam.

CHAPTER 9

Sam didn't wait to be seated. "Jo tells me the dynamite you took from George Simmons is gone. Stolen."

"Right out of our barn," said Clare as she returned with Jesse's shirt. She stopped next to Jesse, who stood near the door. "Let's get this on you."

Together they got the shirt on and Clare buttoned it.

"You know Harry Smith took it." Jesse came farther into the room and sat in one of the light blue Queen Anne chairs on either end of the couch.

Clare, sat on the end of the sofa closest to him and Jo, with baby Paul, next to her.

Sam stood in front of the cold fireplace.

"Clare did you see him take it? Or anyone take it?" he asked.

"No." Her shoulders slumped. "I didn't see anyone."

"Even though we know it was Harry Smith, without some evidence…" Sam shook his head. "There's nothing I can do, Jesse. You know that."

"I know, but I was hoping you'd have a great idea about how to catch him before he uses the dynamite."

"I wish I did, but I don't." Sam sat in the chair at the opposite end of the couch from Jesse. "You've put two guards round the clock at the mine entrance. I think you should increase the crew to three and that third man should be one of my deputies. Then Harry will have to come directly at you if he wants his revenge. I trust my men implicitly. I've worked with all of them for years and have enough to supply one man for each twelve-hour shift. You'll have to pay him in addition to his regular salary from Hope's Crossing."

"Wait, Sam, what do you mean when you say that Harry will have to come directly at Jesse? Are you setting him up as bait?" Clare practically shouted. "Oh, no, you're not. He's weak and injured and can't protect himself. You are not using him as bait. Tell him Jesse."

She waited for Jesse to say something. When she heard nothing, she looked over at him. He had the biggest grin on his face.

"Do you hear that, Sam? My wife already likes me enough to want to keep me around for a while."

"Sure sounds like that to me," agreed Sam.

"Don't you men put any more into her words than is meant to be there," said Jo. "She's just become a bride, for Pete's sake. She doesn't want to be a widow."

"I'm not making her a widow," said Jesse. "I can take care of myself."

Clare sighed and shook her head. "Yes, I can tell that because you always have stab wounds you're healing from and then you greet our friends wearing only your pants."

"All right, admittedly, this looks bad." Jesse pointed at his wounds. "But you got me a shirt so I'm dressed. As to the other, I really can take care of myself otherwise I'd be dead right now."

"He's right," agreed Sam. "George Simmons was a big man but he was fast. I'm surprised Jesse got away with just a few scratches—"

"Scratches!" yelped Clare.

"George was good with that knife," continued Sam. "Preferred that blade to a gun."

"You men are insane." Clare crossed her arms over her chest and slammed herself against the back of the sofa.

Jesse leaned over and put his hand on Clare's knee. "I won't be in any danger. Harry Smith is a coward. He won't confront me."

She didn't see that as any assurance at all. "That only means he's more likely to shoot you in the back."

"Look at me, Clare." He squeezed her leg. "If he meant to do that, he would have by now. He's had four months to plan his revenge or take it against me. But he wants to damage me and make me go out of business, not kill me. He wants me to suffer like he has."

She looked over at him and the earnest expression on his face soothed her fears. "I suppose that's true. You know him better than I do, since I don't know him at all."

"That's right and Sam will make sure

that nothing happens to me."

"As we said earlier, we'll cancel the dinner party tonight," said Clare. "You can't attend in your current state."

"No. I've changed my mind. We'll go on with the festivities as planned," said Jesse.

"But why?" Clare couldn't figure out what her husband was doing now.

"Because the party has been planned for months. Ever since I knew I was getting married."

Her stomach clenched. "To me or to Rebecca Jane?"

"Well, actually since Rebecca Jane. But when she changed her mind—"

"Are you sure she actually changed her mind?" said Clare. She was jealous of a woman she'd never met. Jealous because she had Jesse's affection, whether he realized it or not.

Jesse's eyes narrowed. "You don't know anything about Rebecca Jane or our situation. I suggest you keep your opinions to yourself."

"Certainly. You can do as you please. Jo, you won't have to contact everyone after all. It seems the party is on." She stood and turned to face the three people in the room. "Since I don't have anything else to add to this conversation, I've food to prepare. Sam, Jo, always good to see you."

She stood as straight as she could and walked out of the living room. When she reached the kitchen she went to the counter and leaned on it finally letting her shoulders slump and the tears fall. What did he marry her for anyway? Just someone to warm his bed? He talked about having children, but at this rate she wouldn't have to worry about that. He'd get himself killed long before that day came.

She heard a step behind her.

"I'm sorry, Nora. I'll get busy in a moment."

Hands clasped her shoulders.

"It's not Nora. It's me."

She didn't have the strength to stop Jesse when he pulled her back against him.

"I don't want you to be so upset. Sam is posting deputies at the mine, and he's also posting someone outside our house until Harry Smith is caught. Does that make you feel better?"

She nodded but didn't make a sound, afraid if she did she'd burst into tears.

"Sam and Jo went home. They'll be back later. Come with me upstairs. Lie with me Clare."

After what he said, how can he expect me to lie with him?

He turned her in his arms until she faced him. "Come to bed with me Clare."

She looked up into his face, into his eyes. Desire burned brightly within them. Yet, when he looks at me like this, how can I not?

"Just until you go to sleep. I want you to rest until this party of yours starts."

"All right, commander."

*****

Clare dressed with care in her best outfit, a simple purple dress with lace at the collar and cuffs and white buttons down the front. Nothing fancy, but nice just the same.

She helped Jesse into his suit. He'd keep the coat on so it wouldn't show if he started to bleed again.

"For one night, I can stand it. Sam will see that I sit down when the men go to the office after dinner. It will be fine."

He leaned down and kissed her cheek. "Trust me."

Sam and Jo were the first ones to show

up.

"Are you sure you're up for this?" asked Sam.

"Yes. This is important. I need to see that Clare is a part of our community and as I told her, this has been planned for months," said Jesse.

Clare shook her head and whispered to Jo. "Doesn't he understand this dinner just isn't that important?"

"It is to him," said Jo. "He wants to introduce you to Hope's Crossing and to his...I can't say friends they are mostly his business associates."

The Nelsons, Heidgers and Curt Ames were next, followed by the Morses, Sharecrofts, Jonas Taylor, Ed Regan and Gabe Swanson.

Jesse sat in the office with the rest of the men, talking business. The women were in the parlor. Discussions there ranged from children to favorite recipes.

"You know," said Phyllis Nelson, a very pretty blonde. She had a perfect hourglass figure, probably given her by a wonderful corset. "I've been wondering what the inside of this house looked like. Jesse didn't let anyone see it before you came." She fingered one of the silver candle sticks on the mantle. "It's really quite lovely. I must admit I'm jealous."

"You're jealous of anyone who has something nicer than yours," said Bonnie Heidger, in her forties, was a beautiful brunette with not a strand of gray hair. She and Rich were the oldest of the couples and from what Clare had observed the happiest.

"Which is why, I'm never going to be jealous of you," sniped Phyllis.

"Come now ladies," said Florence Sharecroft. She had perfectly black hair, pulled into a bun on the back of her head. On anyone else, it would have been too severe, but it suited her.

Kate Morse, a bubbly redhead, with hair much lighter and brighter than Clare's, sat on the sofa with Bonnie. Florence sat in one of the wing chairs, Phyllis in the other, when she wasn't walking around touching all the treasures.

"Tell me about Hope's Crossing. Who should I meet?"

"Everyone of any importance is here," said Phyllis.

"Ignore her," said Jo. "Most of the ladies are here. There is also, Effy and Lavernia, the owners of the hotel and mercantile, respectively."

"I met Lavernia. Lovely little lady."

"Effie is just like her. They are both little sweethearts and funny as all get out," added Kate.

"I haven't met Effie yet, but Lavernia is quite funny."

"They both are and they are always feuding with each other," said Florence.

"Yes, Jesse found out today they are twins and seemed quite surprised."

"Twins?! Oh my." Jo laughed. "That explains a lot of things."

All the ladies except Phyllis laughed at this bit of news.

Thirty minutes later, the gentlemen entered the parlor. The dinner party was at an end.

"Thank you for a lovely evening," said Kate. "I haven't had this much fun in a long time. We usually just sit home and read. It's been really nice to get out."

The rest of the ladies echoed Kate's sentiment. Even Phyllis.

"I must say that I did have an enjoyable evening. Thank you both," she gazed at Clare and Jesse, who stood just behind her.

"Thank you all for coming," said Clare.

She felt Jesse's hands at her waist and felt him lean a little against her back. When the last person had left, she quickly closed the door and turned to Jesse. Now that he didn't have a smile painted on his face, she could see the pain he was in.

"Let's go to bed. Lean on me and I'll help you upstairs."

When they arrived in the bedroom, Clare took off Jesse's suit coat and vest. His shirt bore witness that his wounds were open. Both his side and his arm were bloody where his injuries had seeped.

"I have to get some supplies. I'll get new bandages on you and then you can rest. I know you're exhausted."

Jesse nodded. "I'll admit the party took more out of me than I imagined it would."

Before Clare went downstairs, she finished undressing Jesse and got him into bed.

She hurried down the stairs and got new supplies then hurried back upstairs.

Jesse had fallen asleep by the time she arrived. She was loathe to wake him but his wounds needed to be checked.

"Jesse, wake up, please."

He opened his eyes.

"What do you need?"

"Sit up, please, so I can change your bandages.

He nodded and sat up.

She cut through the bandages that wrapped his chest and saw that the pad was not quite soaked but there was still plenty of blood. With quick movements she changed both bandages, cleaning them with soap and water from the basin on the commode. When she was finished, Jesse was white as the sheets on the bed.

"Lie back, sweetheart."

He did and Clare checked his temperature with her wrist on his forehead. He was hot and she was afraid he had a fever.

Clare managed to get Jesse back into bed and covered up.

"I'll return shortly. I need to get some willow bark tea for you."

"Don't leave. Don't leave."

"I'll be right back."

He sighed and waved her away. "Go. I'll be here when you change your mind."

She thought that was an odd thing to say and looked down at him lying against the pillows.

"Jesse?"

He looked at her, eyes so bright with fever, it scared her. Fevers were dangerous and she knew it. Hadn't she almost lost her baby brother to fever just last year?

"Do you know who I am?"

"Of course, I do, Rebecca. We're getting married soon, but I need to rest now." He turned his head on the pillow and closed his eyes. He went to sleep immediately.

Heart racing, Clare ran downstairs.

"Nora. Nora!"

"I'm here," said Nora, wearing her robe and nightgown, coming from her room. "What's the matter?"

"It's Jesse. He's got a fever and he's hallucinating. He thinks I'm Rebecca, the girl he was supposed to marry instead of me."

"All right. I'll bring towels and cold water. You go back up and undress him. Let's see if we can get this fever down."

"I came to get willow bark tea—"

"Water is better. Give him a cool glass full now while I gather the rest of the things we'll need. Then you can give him willow bark tea next time, then water again."

Clare nodded, turned and walked quickly back upstairs.

Jesse had thrown off the covers and was thrashing about.

She filled the glass from the nightstand then sat on the edge of the bed.

"Jesse. It's Clare. Your wife, Clare. Here drink some of this." She reached for the glass and put it to his lips. He gulped eagerly.

Nora appeared with another pitcher of water, a second basin and towels. They each soaked a towel, then wrung it out and laid one towel on his chest and neck above the bandage and one on his stomach below the bandage. As the towels heated, Clare wrung them out in the cool water and replaced them on Jesse's body. Then she and Nora wiped down his arms and legs. Again and again through the night they worked, wiping him down, wringing out the towels in the cool water and wiping him down again. When the water warmed from being on his body they threw it out the window and put fresh cold water in the basin.

Late in the night she sent Nora to bed and she continued to try and cool him. She thought it was working and laid her head on the bed for just a moment to rest.

"Water."

She lifted her head off the bed.

"Water." The voice sounded scratchy, as if not used to talking.

She sat up straight and opened her eyes wide.

"Jesse? Do you know who I am?" She asked the question because she needed to know, but was afraid after last night to hear the answer.

Squinting he nodded. "Clare. My wife."

She grinned. Relief flooded her.

"Yes. Yes, I am. Are you hungry? Would you care for a cup of broth?"

"Please, and water. Lots of water."

Clare could have jumped for joy, but first she had to bring her husband sustenance. She gave him the glass of water.

He downed the entire contents without stopping.

She refilled the glass.

He took only a few gulps this time before handing the glass back.

"Let me get you that broth."

She returned to Jesse's side with a cup of soup and soda crackers.

"Here you are. Sip on this." She handed

him the cup of beef broth.

He was like a starving man, drinking the broth and eating the crackers in nothing flat.

Clare smiled wide. "My goodness, you really are hungry. Could you eat a sandwich and maybe some more soup?"

"Yes, please. Just the sandwich. Then I need to get out of this bed."

He lifted the blankets. "Did you have Sam help get me up here?"

"No, I did it myself. I'm stronger than I look and then I undressed you. Nora and I managed to keep part of you covered all the time. Not an easy feat when the person is in the throes of fever, I can tell you."

"I'm sorry I've been such trouble. My intention was never to have you take care of me."

She thought this an odd thing to say and put her hand to his forehead to check for fever.

"You're my husband. Of course, I'll take care of you. In sickness and in health, remember. Although they could have added in idiocy or not. I still think the plan you and Sam have is risky. I don't like the idea of you being used as bait for someone as dangerous as Smith." She walked toward the door.

"Come, be with me."

She went back to the bed and sat next to him.

He took her hand.

"When I married you, I promised to be and do a lot of things that I can't. Not until this business with Smith is done. Will you wait for me?"

"We've only been married for three days. I probably should have my head examined, but I want this marriage to work, Jesse. I don't want to have to walk away from this."

"I have to do this."

"Maybe you should have Rebecca Jane take care of you next time."

"Rebecca Jane? What does she have to do with this?"

Her mouth in a firm line, Clare debated whether to tell him, but she was the one who'd brought it up.

"When you were in the throes of fever, you called for Rebecca Jane. I know she jilted you, but you still want her."

"You're being ridiculous." He dropped her hand. "Of course I would call for her. She and I were sweethearts for three years until I came out here. Even then we were supposed to get married, but that didn't work out."

"So you got me."

"Yes. So I got you."

His voice was flat, resigned.

Clare knew she was being stupid. There was no way Jesse could have fallen in love with her yet. Just because she started to fall for him the minute he said 'I do' didn't mean he felt the same.

"I'll get your sandwich." She stood. "And I'll help you dress when I return."

He grabbed her hand before she could walk away.

"Clare, thank you."

Feeling his words were only spoken out of obligation, she extricated her hand from his.

"You're welcome." She turned and left the room.

*****

Jesse watched Clare leave. She was so proud. Her back straight as an arrow as she walked away.

He knew he was asking a lot and calling for Rebecca Jane during his fever hadn't helped his cause any. But he had to do this, had to deal with Smith once and for all. The situation could be over soon, if Harry would just take the bait.

Clare returned with his sandwich and handed it to him.

He laid the plate on his stomach.

"Is there anything else I can do for you before I start my chores?"

She stood with her hands clasped in front of her.

"Yes, if you'd help me get dressed I'd appreciate it."

"I know I said I would, but you need to stay in bed."

"I need to get up and make an appearance. I'll go see Sam at his home. That would be the logical thing that I would do and while I'm at Sam's I can lay down for a little while. Then I'll come back home and go back to bed."

She narrowed her eyes. "We just finished with a dinner party that Sam attended. You don't need to go out tonight. Tomorrow will be soon enough."

"All right I'll go tomorrow." He crossed his heart.

Clare took a deep breath and then released it.

"Good. Should I come with you? Maybe we could make it a social call and I could keep an eye on you that way."

"Fine. Social call it is. Now could you get me a shirt, please?"

"I'll find you a nightshirt if you want one."

"I don't own any."

"Then you'll just get ready for bed as usual and if you think I'm changing my mind, you're wrong."

"Harry will come after me. You'll see. Tomorrow we'll go see Sam. I must let the world and Harry in particular, know that I'm well."

CHAPTER 10

Ten days had passed since Jesse was stabbed. Sitting in one of the Queen Anne chairs in the living room he debated with himself, should he or shouldn't he? He was healed and more than capable of making love to his wife.

"Clare, can we talk?"

"Of course." She set her dust rag on the shelf and sat on the sofa next to his chair.

Jesse shook his head and patted his lap. "Sit here."

She cocked her head and nodded.

He thought she would say no but she got up and sat on his legs with her hands clasped in her lap and her back ramrod straight.

He ran his hand up and down her back.

"Relax. I won't bite."

She let out a sigh and relaxed against him.

"Put your arms around my neck."

"Like this?" She wrapped her arms around his neck, bringing her face just inches from his.

"Oh, yes, just like that. Now lower your head just a bit."

"Jesse…just kiss me."

"I thought you'd never ask."

He slanted his mouth over hers and was gratified when she opened for him. Jesse took his time, tasting her lips before his tongue entered her mouth.

"I want to make love to you," he whispered against her lips and covered them again before she could answer.

Finally, she broke off. "I thought you'd never ask," she said with a giggle.

She rose from his lap and took his hand, leading him up the stairs and to their bedroom.

"I know I wanted to wait to make love, but then you got wounded and well, now you're healed and I'm ready to be loved."

Jesse could hardly believe his ears. Had he waited all this time for nothing? Was she just waiting for him to say the words?

They reached the bedroom and Clare led him in, then turned and closed the door behind them. Light from the window illuminated the room, eliminating the need for a lamp.

She walked to him, wrapped her arms around his neck and kissed him, all the while backing up to the bed. Her legs bumped the mattress. She broke the kiss and sat on the bed, patting the spot next to her.

"Sit, please."

He sat and she rose and began taking off his boots. Then she unbuttoned his shirt and ran her hands over his shoulders sliding it down his arms.

She reached for his belt, but he stopped her.

"After you."

Clare smiled and stood. She reached for the buttons on her blouse and slowly undid them, revealing a little more of her chemise with each one. Then she pulled on one of the sleeves and took the garment off, dropping it on top of Jesse's shirt.

Next came her skirt and shoes.

Then she untied the bow on her chemise ribbon and loosened it to mid-chest. She grabbed the bottom and pulled it over her head, but then held it in front of her.

Jesse stood and gently pushed her hands down revealing her to his gaze.

"You're beautiful. Don't hide yourself from me."

"I'm scared," she breathed.

He leaned forward and kissed her. "Don't be afraid. We'll go slowly, and you know I will do my best not to hurt you. I don't want you to focus on what there might be. I want you to feel what is. How do you feel when I do this?" He kissed up and down the column of her neck.

She shivered.

"Or when I do this?"

He nibbled on her ear and then ran his tongue up her neck where he'd just kissed.

"Good. I feel good."

"Wonderful. You're so responsive, Clare. Has anyone ever told you that?"

"Of course, they haven't. You're the first man I've ever kissed."

He chuckled at the irritation in her voice.

"Jesse?"

"Shouldn't we both be undressed for this?"

"Yes, we should."

"Together?"

"Together."

He released her and removed his pants and under drawers.

She removed her bloomers.

"God, Clare you're—"

"Jesse, you're beautiful even with that scar."

"No, sweetheart, you're beautiful." She was the loveliest woman he'd seen in many a while. Perfectly made, with high firm breasts, big enough to fit his hand without overflowing it. Curved in at the waist and flaring at the hips, she was his very own goddess.

"Take your hair down, please. I've dreamed of that red fire flowing around us as I love you."

She reached up and removed the pins holding her hair in place. There was a cascade of dark, rich, red silk down her back to her waist. She brought the mass forward to cover her breasts.

"Gorgeous. I love your hair."

He could see a flush over her skin.

"Thank you."

"But, you mustn't cover these darlings." He swept her hair back over her shoulders.

"Lay on the bed, please."

He watched her lay back on the pillows, her arms at her sides and her body stiff as a board. He came down beside her and rested on his left elbow. With his other hand, he made circles on her stomach, then rubbed fleetingly around her breasts.

"Clare?"

"Yes."

"Relax, sweetheart."

"I am."

He chuckled. "If that's the case I'd like to see you when you're nervous. I could iron my shirts on you."

She smiled, then she giggled and relaxed.

"I guess I am still a little nervous."

He cocked an eyebrow. "Just a little."

"This is difficult for me. I've never…but then you already know that."

"Yes, but we're changing that today. I'm making love to you, Clare. Right here and right now."

He leaned over and kissed her, bringing her to life.

She moaned and squirmed before he finally covered her and made her his.

*****

Clare expected to feel different but she didn't. Not really. Not in any profound way. She'd had a little pain when they joined but otherwise the act was pleasant enough, she supposed.

They lay in bed afterwards, Clare resting her head on Jesse's shoulder.

"Part of that wasn't too bad," she acknowledged while she played with the light dusting of hair on Jesse's chest.

"Only part?"

She heard the smile in his voice. "Yes, the first part was very nice, incredible even."

He chuckled.

"The second part was definitely not as nice."

"Next time you'll like it more. There won't be any pain next time and I'll show you how to move with me."

"I'm definitely willing to learn. Do you think we made a baby today?"

"I don't know. Would that make you happy?"

She looked up at him. "Of course. Wouldn't you be?"

"Yes." He lay with his arm behind his head, flat on his back. His other hand rubbed up and down her back. "I'd be very happy. I want a lot of children. What about you? How many do you want?"

"I don't know. Four or five, maybe."

"I want a dozen."

"A dozen?!" she jerked and stared at him. "I don't know about that. We definitely need to talk more about this."

"I suppose we do, but we can wait until later." He got up and went to the commode, and came back with a damp washcloth. "Here let me take care of you. This will help you feel better."

She looked away. The coolness of the cloth was wonderful and did soothe her. It was worth the embarrassment of lying there with her legs spread wide open while he cleaned her.

"I doubt we really made a baby today," he continued. "I've been told it can take months, or years for a couple to have children."

She nodded and smiled. "I know, and I'll be happy with however many children the good Lord decides to bless us with whether that's one or a dozen."

He took the cloth and placed it back by the basin.

Clare scooted away and out of the bed.

"I still have work to do and I bet you do, too."

"I do, but this was a wonderful interlude."

"I agree. Will we be doing much of that?"

Jesse grinned. "Only as often as I'm capable."

"Oh my. That could be quite often, judging from your physical state right now." She looked warily at his privates as the sheet tented.

"Yes, but no more today. You'll be sore, because it was your first time. Maybe tomorrow, or the next day. We'll see how you're feeling."

"You're a kind man, husband." She was thankful her husband was willing to teach her and not disappointed in her lack of experience. She plucked her clothes off the floor and put them back on. Then she took her hair and redid the bun at the back of her head.

He grinned. "I try, wife."

Jesse got up and dressed. Together, they went down the stairs.

Nora looked up when they entered the kitchen, smiled and went back to chopping vegetables.

*****

They were two months into their marriage and taking Jesse's lunch to him was something Clare looked forward to every day. The errand got her out of the house, onto the back of a horse and into the fresh air. Today was no different. She went out to the barn, saddled her mare, Buttercup, and tied on the saddle bags containing the food.

She walked Buttercup through town and then, when they reached the western end, she let the horse have her head. Buttercup loved to gallop almost as much as Clare did.

Suddenly, Buttercup slid to a stop and Clare, unprepared for the quick halt, went flying over her head. She landed hard on her buttocks and then fell backward and hit her head on a rock. She heard the sound that made Buttercup stop. A rattlesnake. That was the last sound she heard.

*****

"Boss! Jesse! Come on out here!" Bill Johnson called from outside the office.

Jesse stood and walked outside.

"What are you hollering about?"

Bill held an unconscious Clare in his

arms.

"What happened? Hand her to me."

Jesse reached out so Bill could lower Clare into his waiting arms.

"I was riding to work and saw her lying next to the road. Her horse standing well away from her. Her horse apparently spooked when it heard a rattler. The snake was slithering away when I rode up."

"Did it bite her?" He looked down at her for some sign.

"Not that I could tell, but I didn't check her all over. You'll have to do that."

"Fine. Go get Doc Kilarney and have him come here."

"Will do."

Bill leapt onto his horse and galloped out of sight down the trail.

Jesse looked around and called to one of the men standing there. "Tom, help me, please," hollered Jesse. "Go inside and spread one of the blankets from the corner of the room on the floor."

Tom preceded Jesse into the office and held the door open. Then he spread out one of the blankets as Jesse had asked him to.

"Thanks, Tom."

"Sure thing, Boss. You need anything

else."

"No, thank you again."

Tom left the office as Jesse laid Clare on the blanket. He didn't have a sofa to lay her on, but he always kept a couple of blankets in case he ended up sleeping in the office.

He undressed her as quickly as he could and examined her for snake bites. He found none. As he redressed her, he saw Clare awaken.

"Oww." She put her hand to her head. "Jesse?"

"Yes, sweetheart. I'm here."

"Where? I can't see you?"

Jesse waved his hand in front of her open eyes. Nothing.

Dear Lord, she was blind.

"It's all right, Clare. I'm right here. I won't let anyone hurt you."

"Why can't I see you?"

He placed his hand on her shoulder and gently squeezed. "I don't know. The doctor is on his way. We'll know more then. You've hit your head, I'm sure this is only temporary."

Tears formed in her eyes and then rolled down her cheeks.

"What if it's not temporary?" She cried

harder.

Jesse sat beside her and took her into his arms.

"Stop. You're my wife. I want you, no matter the problem. In sickness and in health. Remember?"

Clare wrapped her arms around his waist and cried, her tears wetting his shirt.

"Shh. Don't get worked up. That's not good for you. You're bleeding pretty bad from the injury on the back of your head. I'll get a cloth and some ice for the wound. Now I'm laying you down. I'll be right back."

He laid her back on the blanket and covered her with another. That she couldn't see worried him greatly. He'd never been around someone who'd been blinded by a fall, but Clare would be fine. This was just temporary. He went to the ice box he kept in his office and chipped off chunks of the big block of ice and wrapped them in his unused handkerchief.

"Here now, sit up and let me hold this on your wound. You just lean on me."

Thirty minutes after Bill left to get him, Dr. Kilarney hurried through the door.

"Let me see her, Jesse."

Jesse was relieved the doctor was finally

there. "She's blind, Doc."

Doc examined her wound and felt around for any others he couldn't see. "Clare, how do you feel, besides the wound on the back of your head? Do you have a headache? Where does it hurt?"

"Yes, I…I do. It's right behind my eyes. It's pounding like I can feel my blood coursing through my veins." She sniffled but didn't cry. "I'm blind, Doc. Will I stay this way?"

Doc hesitated. "I don't think the blindness will be permanent. You've jarred your retina loose and the blindness is the result of that. Once everything settles back down and your retina tightens itself again, I believe your vision will return. In the mean time, to encourage your healing, you need to rest and try to relax. I'm bandaging your eyes closed. I don't want you to strain your eyes. I'll remove the bandage in about ten days and see if we need to put it back on or not." The doctor took her hand. "I know this is difficult. You're scared and you hurt, but I do believe that you will be fine."

Jesse squeezed her hand. "I'm hooking up the buckboard we use to carry ore and taking you home," said Jesse.

"I'm sorry Jesse, so very sorry," wept Clare.

"Here now, there is no need to be sorry." He's sad she feels the need to apologize. What kind of man does she think he is? What kind of man has he been? "Accidents happen. I just want you to get better and that means taking it easy for a while."

"Yes, that is just what the doctor ordered," said Doc.

He looked at Jesse and shook his head and then lifted his shoulders.

Jesse's stomach clenched.

Doc wasn't sure she'd recover.

Closing his own eyes, Jesse held her close and put his head on top of hers. Clare was a strong woman, she'd get through this, but he knew these first few days would be difficult. Oh, he'd have Nora to help him, but Jesse still had to oversee the mining operations. Bill Johnson had proved to be trustworthy. He brought Clare to Jesse when he could have left her. He should be rewarded for that.

Jesse made Bill a manager with the responsibility of coming to the Donovan's every day with his report and those of the other managers, too.

For now Jesse had to concentrate on helping Clare to recover her vision, if it was even possible.

*****

Harry watched from the deep gully that hid him and his horse from the passersby on the road. He'd had it all worked out. The snake rattles were still in his hand. He'd shaken them just as Donovan's wife rode past on her way to the mine, just like she did every day. Carrying his lunch to him like a good little wife.

Instead of her horse rearing like he expected, the dang critter had stopped dead in its tracks, sending her flying over his neck.

He'd wanted her unconscious so that was good. Just as he started out of the gulch, Bill Johnson came riding up, stopped and scooped up the woman.

All Harry could do was watch, cursing that his plan was ruined.

When he was sure Bill was long gone, Harry came out of the ravine and headed down the mountain to tell his boss the bad news. He really didn't want to say anything. The boss had a terrible temper but the punishment would be all the worse for him if he didn't relate what happened.

He dismounted in front of the big house on the North side of town. When he reached the front porch he took off his hat and began rolling the brim in his fingers. Finally, he knew he couldn't put it off any longer and knocked.

Phyllis Nelson opened the door.

"Good afternoon, Boss."

CHAPTER 11

Jesse carried Clare to the buckboard and took her home. When they arrived, he carried her upstairs to bed where he undressed her.

"I'm getting pretty good at this." He smiled and then realized she couldn't see him, which made him frown.

"At what?"

She looked to where his voice was, almost like she could see him.

"At undressing you. I had to do it earlier to check for snake bites."

Clare slowly nodded. "That's why Buttercup stopped so suddenly, she heard a snake." She started to rise from the bed.

"Buttercup? How is she? Did she get bit? Is she all right?"

Jesse put a hand on her shoulder. "The horse is fine. Now, as much as I am revolted by this nightgown, by any nightgown which keeps your luscious body from me, I have to put it on you, since you'll be in bed for the next few days and will probably have visitors. I know you like your modesty."

"Thank you. You're right I'm a modest person in most circumstances. And if you are so revolted by this nightgown, buy me one you are not revolted by."

He sat on the bed and held her hand. "I'll consider it. Now that you're settled, what can I get for you? We missed lunch are you hungry?"

"No. I just want some water with laudanum for my head."

"The doctor said no laudanum because you have a head injury, but I can give you willow bark tea. Would you like some?"

She tugged the sheet up under her arms. "Yes, please."

"All right, I'll be back in one swish of a horse's tail." He stood and walked to the door, turned and looked back at his wife. She lay there in bed, helpless and crying silently, the tears making trails down her beautiful face.

Her tears tore him up inside, but he'd never let her know. She had every right to cry, more than she knew.

He came back in a short while with the tea.

"Here you go. Drink it carefully. It's very hot."

Jesse guided her hand to the cup and helped her take a hold of it.

"Do you want me to help you?"

"Yes, please. I don't think I'd enjoy spilling hot liquid down my front."

He took the cup and held it next to her lips, tilting it very slowly until the liquid touched her she sipped. He did it a couple of times before he asked, "Is that enough for now?"

"Yes. I'll drink the rest of it after it's cool. For now, I could use some water, if you wouldn't mind."

"Of course, I don't mind. I'm yours to command."

He filled her glass with cool water from the pitcher on the bureau. Then he sat again and held the glass to her lips. She took hold of it and drank. When she'd had enough she held it out for Jesse to take from her.

"I think I'd like to rest now. The willow bark tea seems to be helping some."

"Do you want me to lie down with you?"

She shook her head then raised her hand to her temple. "Oww, I must remember not to do that. But, no. You have things to do. You don't need to lie with me."

He shook his head, again forgetting that she couldn't see him. "You are the most important thing on my agenda until you get well."

"That could take a long time. Maybe never. I'm not a fool. I know there is a possibility, even a probability, that I won't ever recover my eyesight. I need to come to grips with that fact and so do you. Our neighbor back home had the same thing happen. He fell while plowing and landed face first on a rock. He went blind too and stayed blind for the short time that he lived."

"Your injury is nothing like that, but I won't lie to you." He had to swallow hard before speaking again. "The doctor doesn't know if this is permanent or not. He's heard of people who never recover their vision and others that can see again in a few days. You will be one of those people." He patted her shoulder. "I know it."

"But you don't know," she spat the words at him. "Nobody knows."

Jesse knew she wasn't angry with him, just with the situation, but hearing the anger in her voice was still hard.

"I'll have Nora make us some sandwiches. You've got to keep up your strength."

"I don't feel weak. I feel blind."

The last words were shouted.

He lifted his hand from her shoulder.

Clare sat propped against the pillows on the bed, her hands resting in her lap.

Jesse put his hand over hers.

"I know you're scared, but we'll get through this. Give it time."

"Yes, I'm scared. I don't know what to expect. I don't know if I'll ever be whole again. Why don't you order a replacement bride for me?"

Jesse knew she was feeling sorry for herself. She was allowed. He could only imagine what was going through her mind.

"I want the bride I've got." He cringed at that word and wish he'd never said it. Clare was not his replacement bride any longer. She was the bride he was supposed to have. "Your blindness doesn't change that. We'll work around it."

"How will we work around the fact that I can't see?"

He squeezed her hands as they lay on her lap. "Well, to begin with you'll learn where everything is so you can get around by yourself. I'll make you a cane so you can tell what is in front of you and avoid collisions."

Clare cried again, the tears following the same tracks down her cheeks.

"What's the matter? Why are you crying now?"

"You're being so nice to me. Why?"

Jesse rolled his eyes, thankful the gesture was unseen by Clare. "Because you're my wife. I want you to stay my wife, and I need to help you for that to happen. If I don't, you're liable to find a way to leave and I don't want that."

"How can I leave? I can't even find my way to the chamber pot without feeling my way there."

"We'll work it out. You can have me help you or Nora can, whoever you prefer."

"I want you. What if I wake in the

middle of the night? You can't be waking Nora at all hours."

"That's fine. I'll do it."

"I think the tea is taking effect. I don't want to talk about this anymore. I need to sleep now. Maybe when I wake up…"

She didn't finish the sentence. Both of them knew what she wanted; to have her sight back when she woke.

Jesse was sure that wouldn't happen and the situation saddened him.

*****

Clare awoke in the dark, blinked her eyes and then she remembered. She was blind and seeing only black.

She felt a warm body at her back. "Jesse?"

His arm came around her and pulled her close. "I'm here."

"You slept with me?"

"You needed me here with you. As soon as I laid down, you scooted next to me. Admit it, you've grown used to me in the two months we've been married."

She sighed. "I suppose I have. Is it night time?"

"No, just late afternoon. Do you need to get up?"

"No. I'm fine."

"I'll get you a cane now if you'll be all right by yourself. I'm sure I can make one if the mercantile doesn't have any."

She gripped his hand. "Please make it. I'm not ready for the whole town to know my business."

"All right, I'll make you one. It'll be ready for when Dr. Kilarney says you can get out of bed."

"I hope that's soon. I'm already tired of being in bed."

He held her tighter. "I know, but you must rest. You have to give whatever came loose the chance to get back into place."

"I know."

"Come here, and relax with me. It's not all bad being in bed, as long as you share it with me. Is it?"

She smiled. "No, being in bed with you is not all bad." She giggled.

"That's an ornery thing to say." But he chuckled. She was trying to find her sense of humor and that was a good thing.

*****

Clare tried to sleep but every time she closed her eyes she saw the same blackness as when they were open. Jesse was being so kind to her, there at her side whenever she needed him. Jesse would be giving her baths and helping her to the privy every day. She was totally dependent on him and she didn't like it one little bit.

On the second day after the accident, Doc Kilarney came to visit.

"Clare, I've been doing more reading on conditions like yours and I'm even more sure that your vision will return if you rest and relax. No jarring of the head, don't get excited or upset, be calm and your vision will return in the next few weeks."

"I'll make sure she relaxes," said Jesse.

Clare sighed. "If you think it will work, Doc, I'll stay in bed, though laying here is my least favorite thing to do."

"Have Jesse or Nora read to you. Sleep. Really try to take it easy."

"All right, Doc. I'll do my best."

The doctor took her hand in his. "And keep your spirits up."

"That's a harder request to keep."

"We'll be fine. I'll make sure," said Jesse.

"All right," said the doctor. "I'll be back day after tomorrow to check your vision again. Let me know if there are any changes.

If you have headaches or anything you don't have right this minute."

"See you then, I hope." Clare turned over toward the wall. She heard Jesse and the doctor leave and walk down the stairs. They were talking but so softly she couldn't hear what they said.

A few minutes later Jesse returned. She knew his scent. Sandalwood and something that was unique to him.

"What can I do for you?"

"Nothing."

"Good. We'll read."

"Didn't you hear me? I said I don't want anything. I just want to be left alone."

She heard his boots as he crossed the floor and then felt the bed sag as he sat.

"Clare," he said as he scooted closer to her. "I'm not leaving, so you can continue to be ill-tempered or you return to being the sweet woman that I know you to be."

"You don't understand." She paused, "You think I'm sweet?"

"Yes."

She heard the smile in his voice.

"I think you're sweet."

His breath was on her neck and then he kissed her. She was super sensitive since she couldn't see. She felt his soft kiss all the way to her toes.

"And gentle."

He kissed her again.

She angled her neck so he had better access.

"And kind."

He kissed her neck again, moving down with each kiss.

She moaned.

"Do you like what I'm doing?"

"Yes, you know I do."

"I want you to feel me, to know me by nothing more than my touch. Do you want to try?"

She thought about it for a moment. "Yes. I'd like to try."

Jesse moved the blankets off of her body.

She lay still, waiting for him to kiss her again. She flinched when he took her foot in his hand. He massaged the bottom, around the top and over the ankle. He pulled on each of her toes and then rubbed each one.

The sensations were amazing. She couldn't see him and yet she seemed to feel his movements intensely.

He moved up to her calf and then her

thigh, massaging as he moved ever forward. Around and around, back and forth, up and down. With each movement she felt herself relax a little more.

"Lift your hips for me," he said softly

She did and her nightgown was bunched around her waist. He continued to massage her legs.

"Sit up now and then raise your arms."

She lifted them and he pulled her gown up and over her head. Clare was now naked as the day she was born.

All her senses concentrated on the movement of his hands on her skin.

"Now, I want you to turn over onto your stomach, please."

Clare rolled over, towards the middle of the bed so she didn't fall off her side.

"Scoot back toward me and then rest your head on the pillow."

She responded to each request, feeling every touch, every breath on her skin.

Jesse started rubbing her back, just as she'd done his a few weeks ago.

"Relax, Clare. Feel me."

He kissed a trail down her back and then licked the same path back up, his breath hot on her skin.

His hands smoothed over her back and down her sides, rough on her tender skin.

"Do you like this?"

He moved his hands away.

"Do you want me to stop?"

"No," she cried out. "Don't stop."

"Shh."

His hands were upon her again and she relaxed, her breathing ragged. He soothed her, reaching all those places she couldn't.

Clare had never felt anything so incredible. No wonder her father had liked for her mother to do this for him. Or that Jesse had liked when she massaged him that other night. Had it really been nearly two months ago?

"Jesse, this feels so wonderful. I don't want you to ever stop."

"I've got to stop, love. I'm removing my clothes and you and I are taking a nap together. I'm holding you in my arms and touching you. I'm bound to make love to you unless you stop me."

"Don't you think that would be too much movement? I don't think Doc would be pleased." Excitement and fear warred within her.

"Then I'll just continue to touch you,

and then I'll hold you. But you may be right, I don't want our love-making to be anything but good memories. There should never be any fear, even of the unknown."

"Since you've decided not to replace me, and we should know in a few days whether this will be permanent or not. We can wait until then to make love."

"Yes, we can wait until you get your vision back."

She wanted to tell him that no, they'd make love now, vision or not, but she was afraid, so afraid that any excitement could keep her blind.

They could wait for a few days. What would a few days matter?

Clare again felt the bed shift as Jesse rose to remove his clothes and then he was beside her. He brought the blankets with him and covered them both before taking her in his arms and holding her. Just holding her.

He didn't make any demands or rush to make love to her before she changed her mind. He simply nestled her back against his chest and wrapped his arms around her.

"How's that? Comfortable?"

"Mmm. Yes. I'm warm again, too."

He chuckled.

She pictured his smile.

How long before she didn't remember what his smile looked like…what he looked like? How long before she forgot everything? The color of the sky in the morning, the full moon at night.

She tried so hard to have hope, but sometimes the sadness overwhelmed her. What if she could never see her children? Tears formed and she couldn't stop them from falling.

"Clare? Why are you crying?"

"I'll never see our children. I won't watch them grow up, get married and have children of their own. How long before I forget what you look like or what color the sky is at twilight?"

He pulled her closer and held her tight.

"None of that will happen. You'll get your sight back. You'll see. I prom—"

"You can't promise. You can't fix this, Jesse. No one can."

"Perhaps not, but I can do my damndest to keep you calm. To keep you from injuring yourself further. Please Clare, this is not good for you." He braced a hand on her head to keep her still. "Sweetheart, please try to calm down."

Clare stopped, sure she'd misheard.

"Did you just call me sweetheart?"

"I might have."

She imagined he looked at her, his chest bare, smiling.

"Would you like it if I did?"

She started to nod and then thought better of it. "Yes, I'd like it very much."

"Then sweetheart it is."

"I can hear the smile in your voice."

"Is that a bad thing? I'll work on not smiling when I talk to you."

"No, don't stop. Smiling is a very good thing."

A knock sounded on the door downstairs and then there were pounding footsteps as someone hurried up to them.

The mattress shifted.

"Clare?" called Sam.

"Sam?"

"And Jo and Paul, we just don't move as fast as he does," said Jo.

Clare pulled the sheets around her naked form. "It's awfully nice of you to come and see me...even if I can't see you back." She looked up to where she thought Jesse would be. "Are you dressed? Or are you greeting our guests in the all-together?"

"I have my pants on and now I'm getting my shirt, Mrs. Smarty Pants."

"Maybe you could help me dress and we could meet them downstairs…"

"No," said all three of them at once.

"You're not to get out of this bed for the next three days at least," said Jesse.

"Yes, when Doc stopped by and told us what happened," said Jo. "He said you were to get all the bed rest you could."

Clare looked to where she thought Sam was standing. "What about you Sam? I haven't heard from you?"

"Same as Jo said. I can see by the way you move toward the sound that you're using all your senses. Now that one is incapacitated, your others, hearing, touch and I would bet that your senses of taste and smell are becoming more acute."

"I…I don't know. I've been feeling so sorry for myself that I haven't paid much attention... until you just mentioned them. I think you may be right though. Even at this distance I can smell that little Paul needs a diaper change." She grinned imagining Jo lifting the baby and sniffing his diaper.

"You're right. If you gentlemen will leave for a moment, I'll help Clare into her night clothes and change Paul's diaper."

"We'll be right outside if you need us," said Jesse.

Clare heard the click of the men's boots on the floor as they crossed the room and went out the door.

"Where do you want me?" she asked Jo.

"Let me put Paul on the floor. He's starting to crawl. Now come to the side of the bed and sit. Did we break up something? I know our timing can be off."

"No, it's fine. Jesse was just trying to comfort me. We didn't because the doctor thinks I should remain still and not have any jarring of my head or any anxiety or exertion."

Jo snorted. "Doc told us that same thing and said we were to make sure you stayed as still and calm as possible. That definitely leaves out making love."

Clare laughed. "That's what I was telling Jesse. How is your sweet baby? I wish I could see him. I bet he's growing like a weed."

"He is and when you get your sight back you'll see exactly how much. Lift your arms."

Clare obeyed.

Jo slid the nightgown over her head.

"Lift your hips and I'll pull it down."

"I haven't been up on my feet yet. Jesse carried me up here and I've been putting off taking care of business, but I could really use your help to do it now."

"Sure. Take hold of my arm."

Jo helped Clare stand and then Clare put her hand on Jo's arm. Jo led the way behind the screen. Afterwards she helped Clare back to the bed.

"While you're standing, let me put on your dressing gown."

Jo slid one sleeve on and then helped with the other and tied the belt around her waist.

"Now let me change Paul then I'll go get the men."

Clare heard her walk across the room and get the baby. Then she was back and she felt the mattress dip a little as she laid the baby down to change his diaper. She made quick work of changing the baby's diaper for it was just a few minutes later when she said, "Here, you hold him while I get Jesse and Sam."

"Oh, no. I couldn't. I can't see."

"You're blind, not crippled. You can

still feel what he's doing. You know how to hold a baby, that hasn't changed."

The next thing Clare knew, the baby was touching her chest and she automatically put up her hands to hold him. She took him under his little arms and held him at what she thought was eye level then leaned forward and touched his tummy with her nose. Clare rubbed his belly and made noises. She was so thrilled when he giggled that she laughed, too.

"See. I told you that you know how to hold a baby."

Jo sounded like she was across the room. "Are you all here? How long have you been watching?" asked Clare.

She heard boots coming toward her.

"Long enough to hear Paul giggle." Jesse sat next to her. "You're so good with him, with or without sight."

She felt him lean into her, then he whispered in her ear. "I can't wait to see you with our babes or to enjoy making them with you."

Jo laughed. "I don't know what you two are talking about but whatever it is, stop. Clare is red clean to the top of her head. Ah, and now Jesse is, too."

Clare couldn't stop herself from blushing, but loved knowing that her handsome husband blushed, as well.

"Jo, you better come get Paul. I think I'll lie down again. Please pull up chairs or sit on the bed. Don't leave, it's just my head is hurting a bit."

"Maybe we should let you get some rest," said Sam.

"Ah, I was wondering if you came back in, too. Did you take the rest of the day off?" asked Clare, looking in the direction of Sam's voice.

"No, this is business as well as social."

"What is your business?" asked Clare.

"I want to know if your accident could have been anything other than an accident," said Sam.

"If you mean did someone want me to fall and kill myself, I don't think so. I don't remember seeing anyone around and Bill..." She patted Jesse's leg. "Isn't that who you said found me?"

"Yes," Jesse answered. "Bill Johnson. He said he found a snake slithering off when he got there."

"But there were no bite marks?" asked Sam.

"I checked as soon as I could and there weren't any signs that she'd been bitten."

Sam took a deep breath. "I don't know. I'm trying to figure out if there is anything else we should be looking at here."

"I don't see any nefarious motive for him bringing Clare to me. If he'd wanted to harm her all he had to do was leave her there. And he didn't know I'd promote him. He's a good man, Sam," said Jesse.

"All right," said Sam. "I'll take your word for that. I want to make sure we keep you and Clare safe. I just don't know what Harry Smith may be planning. It's been nearly two months since any incidents. Do you think he could have left town?"

"I doubt that he's left town. I think he's just biding his time, but I'll be here for Clare and if I'm not Nora is." Jesse pointed out, "she won't be left alone."

"Good. That's good," said Sam.

"Would you and Jo like to stay for supper?" asked Jesse.

"I think we'll come back another time," said Jo. "Clare doesn't need to be playing hostess, or even thinking that she should be. As a matter of fact, we've over-stayed our welcome. Clare needs to rest."

"Thank you both for coming by, but I think Jo may be right. I'm feeling tired and do need to lie down." Clare slouched.

She heard two sets of boots stop in front of her.

"Feel better soon." Sam kissed the top of her head.

"Yes, and next time we come, you'll have your vision back," said Jo, she kissed Clare's cheek.

"Thanks, you two. I'll definitely see you next time." Clare waited until she heard them all going down the stairs before scooting to the edge of the bed, standing and moving to take off her dressing gown.

"You need some help with that?" asked Jesse from across the room.

She jumped and closed the dressing gown back around her.

"I thought you went downstairs with Jo and Sam."

"They are perfectly capable of showing themselves out of our house."

She heard him walk toward her and felt his hands upon her shoulders as he took the garment and slid it off her arms.

Clare backed up to the bed and sat before swinging her legs up and lying down.

"My head hurts."

"I bet it does. Do you want some willow bark tea?"

"Yes, please."

"All right, I'll be right back."

Clare turned on her side, away from the door. Is this what she had to look forward to for the rest of her life? How long before Jesse got tired of her and looked for another replacement bride?

CHAPTER 12

Two weeks passed and a little change occurred in Clare's vision. She thought she might be seeing more light but she still couldn't make out shapes or faces. Mostly what she saw was not solid black, now it was gray. She hoped that was a positive sign, but she wasn't ready to say anything to anyone about it.

She heard Jesse's boots cross the floor toward the bed where Clare lay propped up with pillows. She knew the rhythm of his steps now.

"Clare."

"Yes."

"I have to go into work."

"I know you can't stay with me forever. Please, help me get dressed before you go. That's one less thing Nora will have to worry about."

"Sure. What do you want to wear?"

She pictured her wardrobe in her mind.

"The purple dress I think. It's my favorite."

"Mine, too. The color makes your red hair shine."

She smiled. "That's nice to hear."

"I guess I don't tell you often enough how good you look."

"It's all right. I can't see myself anyway, but it's always nice to hear a compliment."

Jesse's arms wrapped around her and he pulled her back against him before whispering in her ear.

"I've been remiss. Whether you can see or not, I should tell you how beautiful you are everyday."

"Oh, no, not every day." Clare laughed. "There are sure to be days where I look a mess and you should tell me that as well."

"We'll see."

He placed a kiss on her temple and released her.

"Let me get that dress then I'll take you downstairs. This is only your second day out of bed. You can keep Nora company today."

"All right."

She didn't really think that Nora wanted her company, but she could sit in the parlor as easily as she could sit up in bed and Nora wouldn't have to climb up and down the stairs to bring her food and drink.

Jesse got her situated on the sofa in the parlor.

"Is there anything you need before I leave?"

"I don't think so. You've put a glass of water on the table where I can reach it, right?"

"Yes, let me show you."

He took her hand and placed it where the glass sat on the table next to her.

"Then I'm fine. You go on to work and don't worry about me."

She heard him cross the room to the front door and leave through it. Clare brought her feet up and laid her head against the padded arm of the sofa. She was so tired.

Clare awoke with a start. She didn't know what had awakened her but she knew something was definitely wrong. There was a smell in the room…

"Nora. Nora!"

"Nora, ain't coming boss man's lady," said a gravely man's voice.

Clare turned toward the sound.

"Who are you and what do you want here?"

"I'm Harry Smith, and I came for you. Though whether that husband of yours will pay ransom for a blind wife or just call it a relief that you're gone, is yet to be seen."

Clare's stomach clenched. "Ransom?" She stalled for time. "Are you planning on taking me somewhere?"

"Yes, you're going with me—"

"Never." She slyly reached for the cane that Jesse made for her and she kept next to the sofa.

"You didn't let me finish. You'll come with me to keep me from doing to Nora or perhaps Jo Longworth, the same that was done to you. Who knows if a blow to the head would kill either one of them or just make them blind like you? And Jo with that little baby to take care of. Tsk. Tsk. You can prevent that by coming with me without makin' a fuss."

Clare unwrapped her hand from the

cane. She wouldn't risk Jo or Nora. "You're insane, Harry. Jesse will never ransom me. I'm blind remember? Who wants a blind wife." She knew this wasn't true. Jesse had been nothing but kind to her since her accident. She thought they might actually be getting closer, but that was why she had to make Harry believe that Jesse didn't want her.

"He'd better. Now it's time for you to shut up. Give me your hands."

Harry tied her hands together in front of her.

"And I can't have you screaming your fool head off either, so..."

He gagged her with a cloth and then he pulled her by her hands out to a wagon he had waiting. Here he put her in the back of the wagon and covered her with a blanket. No one would see her.

She felt absolutely helpless. She didn't know for certain how long they traveled or which way.

He helped her down from the wagon and then tugged her hands. They walked maybe fifteen or twenty feet.

"There's two steps up."

She gingerly extended her shoe and then

mounted the stairs.

Harry pulled her over a small porch and then across a threshold. He finally stopped and pushed her down onto a bed.

"You stay there, not that you could go anywhere."

He'd pulled her into what she assumed was a house. When she looked up, she saw the door wide open with a shiny brass-colored padlock on the outside.

Wait. She saw? Saw? Her vision was back. She bit back a gasp of joy. The images weren't crystal clear, but she could see shapes and colors. She knew Harry was a brown-haired man with a beard.

Apparently, the gray she'd been seeing at home was now giving way to full-fledged vision. Not clear vision, but she could see. Her heart pounded and her pulse raced. She'd be able to see her beloved Jesse if she got out of this mess alive. Clare was careful not to let Harry know so she didn't end up blindfolded...or dead.

"There you go now, boss man's lady. This here place is my home away from home. No one has ever been here 'cept me and the boss, so no one will find ya here. I don't want to have to kill ya. At least, that ain't my intent."

"What is your intent, Mr. Smith? What is it you really want? What are you trying to achieve with these violent measures you're taking?"

"I'm trying to put your husband out of business, that's what."

"Why? What will that achieve except to put hundreds of people out of work?"

"Everybody will leave and my boss can claim the mine. Then I'll be the one who is rich, too, 'cause the boss has said I can own part of the mine."

Clare shook her head, very gingerly, hopefully not enough that Harry would realize how gently she was being.

"That is crazy. Neither you or your boss will ever be the owner of the mine, it would not be legal. Besides, there is too much gold for anyone, my husband or any of the other miners to stop production over your attacks, no matter how many times you blow it up. They'll just dig it out and start up again."

She watched as Harry sat in one of the chairs at the small square table. "Well, in the mean time, I'll get even with that husband of yers. He didn't have no call to fire me."

"Come now Harry, be realistic. You

came to work drunk and caused two men grievous injuries. They have to work in the company store now, no longer capable of working in the mine, because of you. Jesse couldn't keep you on after that."

"At least they're workin'. No mine in these hills will hire me 'cause of yer husband."

"You brought that on yourself and you know it. That's why you're so angry."

"Just hush up, afore I hit ya."

Clare immediately shut up. She didn't want her newly returned vision to go away maybe for good if he hit her, besides the fact that his blow would hurt.

"Now. Since I never learned how to read and write, yer goin' to write a ransom note for me."

"How am I supposed to do that when I can't see?"

"I thought about that. I figured I'd just set yer hands on the paper and give you a pencil. I'll tell you when to stop and then I'll move yer hand down to the next line. It'll work fine."

"Since I don't have much choice, let's get to it." She held out her hand toward his voice.

"What do you want me to do with yer hand now? I ain't got the paper yet."

"I'm blind, Mr. Smith. You'll have to lead me where you want me to write the note. You have a table or counter, or some flat surface, I assume."

He scratched his head. "Yeah. I got a table I'll take you to."

Smith took her hand and pulled her to her feet. Then he put her arm through the crook of his elbow and led her to the small, square table with three wooden slat-back chairs around it.

"Here you go. The table is in front of you and there's a chair to your right side."

He took one of her hands and put it on the table and then placed her other one on the chair.

She released his hand as quickly as possible, hating to touch the vile man, and pretended to fumble into the chair as she thought she would have done if she was still without sight.

Actually, writing the note would be easier the way he said, since she didn't have perfect vision yet and could see things that were far away easier than those that were close.

"The paper is here."

He put her left hand on the sheet of paper and her right on the pen.

"I got a pen 'stead of a pencil. That'll look more serious. The inkwell is in front of where the pen is."

Smith moved her hand so it touched the inkwell.

"Start writin'."

She used her right hand in a tapping motion to find the inkwell and then her left to hold the well and dip the pen.

"You'll have to show me the edge of the paper again."

He did.

"What would you like to say?"

"Write this."

Donovan,

Bring $10,000 in gold to the old Hopper place by day after tomorrow at sundown or your wife dies.

Harry Smith

"Is this the old Hopper place, Mr. Smith?"

She knew that Harry couldn't read but thought he could probably recognize his own name and the numbers, so she wrote:

Donovan,

My sight is restored, but I haven't let him know. I am at the Hopper place waiting, he wants $10,000 in ransom for me.

Harry Smith

"Does it look all right, Mr. Smith?"

"Yeah, that's great. I'm takin' this and leavin' it at yer house, where he'll find it. If I'm lucky I won't have to tie up yer cook again."

She sucked in a breath. "You didn't hurt her did you?"

Harry crossed the room.

Clare was careful not to follow him with her eyes, and to only turn her head toward him after he'd spoken.

"I didn't do no permanent damage. Just knocked her out, then tied her up and put her in the pantry. She'll have a headache but other than that, she'll be fine. Do you think Donovan has come home yet?"

"My guess would be no. But I don't know how long he was to be gone. This was his first day back to work since my accident."

Harry threw back his head and laughed.

"What's so funny?"

"T'wernt no accident you gettin' thrown like that. I was in the gully waiting for you to come bringing his lunch like you did every day."

"You did this to me? But I thought—"

"I didn't mean for you to go blind. I just wanted you to fall off your horse so I could nab you, but then that Bill Johnson came by and picked you up. That no good do-gooder ruint my plans."

"Bill saved my life."

"I wouldn't a let you die. Now, you just be a good girl. I'm gonna tie you back up and lock you in this here house so nothing kin happen to ya."

"What could happen to me? I'm blind. It's not like I'm leaving any time soon."

He picked up the rope and tied her hands, then took the letter and put it in his coat pocket. "Probably true, but I ain't takin' no chances."

Harry walked to the door. "Bye, now."

She turned toward the sound of his voice.

He walked out the door.

She heard the key turn in the lock. As soon as she was sure he was gone, she jumped up and ran to the window to see where she was. Her vision wasn't clear yet, but even so, she knew she was in trouble when all she could see from the small window was a little bit of the clearing the house sat in and then trees. No other houses were in sight.

Clare sat on the sofa and used her teeth on the knot at her hands. If she could get it loose…slowly she worked pulling the rope free. She got the first knot undone and worked on the second. Finally, she was free.

The window was too small to crawl out of so she looked around the room for something she could use to get out the door, to pry it loose or break the lock. There was a kitchen area with a counter and a couple of shelves above it on one wall, the iron bedstead on another wall, the fireplace on the third and the door to the outside along with the table and chairs on the last wall. The room was small only about ten feet by ten feet with only the one door.

She went to the kitchen and looked for a knife. Surely if Smith was living here then he would have utensils to eat with. A wooden bucket sat on one end of the counter. In it were dirty dishes. Plate, bowl, cup, and a knife, fork, and spoon. She grabbed the knife and went back to shove the blade between the door and the latch, trying to wedge it open. The knife bent. Clare kicked the door and then cursed because now her toe hurt. She threw the knife back in the bucket and prayed he didn't decide to wash the dishes until after Jesse had come for her.

Not knowing how far this cabin was from town, she kept a watchful eye on the window, checking outside every few minutes.

Finally, she saw him returning. Apparently this house wasn't very far from town at all, assuming he took the ransom note to her house as he'd said and not to the mine. But, of course, he did. Too many people were at the mine who would recognize him if he rode in.

She quickly sat back in the chair where he'd left her. She grabbed the rope and put it loosely around her wrists and held the ends in her closed fists. Hearing the key turn in the lock she turned toward the door. She let the door shut before speaking, keeping up her ruse.

"You're back. Did you take the note to my house? Were you able to leave it, or was Jesse home?"

"The boss man wasn't home and yer

cook was still in the pantry, so I just waltzed in and left the note on yer kitchen table. I didn't dawdle none, 'cause I didn't know when he'd be home."

Poor Nora, but at least he didn't hurt you again. "You're back quicker than I expected you to be."

"That's the beauty of this place. Most people didn't know the Hopper's so they don't know about this little place."

"If that's true, how will Jesse know where to find me?"

"Oh, he was one of the few that were here then. All the big mine owners were. Fact is, the Nelsons bought the Hoppers' claim when they left. It showed color about six months later and they hit the mother lode another two months after that."

"Nelsons? Phyllis and Will?"

"One and the same."

"Did the Hopper's ever know their claim proved out?"

"Doubt it. They was headed to California. The old lady's brother was some kind of farmer and they went to help him. 'Sides that, don't make no difference. They sold it fair and square."

Clare continued to keep her eyes from

focusing on him, or anything, if she could help it. That was all she needed, for him to decide to get rid of her because she'd seen too much. Though she couldn't imagine what she wasn't supposed to see.

A knock sounded on the door.

She turned her head toward the sound and had to bite back a gasp.

The door opened. Standing there was Will Nelson, one of Jesse's friends and a fellow mine owner.

"Come on in, Boss."

CHAPTER 13

Nelson entered the room. She knew him from the dinner party. He towered over Harry by a good six to eight inches.

"Well, I see you managed to get Clare without any trouble," he said to Harry. "After you talked to Phyllis, I wasn't sure you'd be able to."

Clare kept her vision on Will's stomach, not daring to look up for fear he would know she could see. As the time passed her vision was clearer and clearer. Now it was almost back to normal.

"Will? Is that you?"

"Still can't see, huh, Clare?"

She ignored his question. "What are you

doing here, Will?"

"This is my operation."

"But, why?" *How could I have hosted these people in my home?* "What did Jesse ever do to you? I thought you were his friends."

"Phyllis and I were never Jesse's friends. His mine produces more than ours so we have to have it. It's that simple. Profits, my dear Clare. Profit is what motivates us. Well, it's what motivates Phyllis. Keeping her happy is what motivates me."

If she could have stopped herself from the flush of anger she would have. As it was she felt the tell-tale heat in her cheeks. "Jesse will stop you. He's bringing your ransom. He'll do what you asked."

"Don't be so sure. I wouldn't. But then I'm not Jesse who I would guess is rather taken with you."

"Why would you say that? I'm just a mail-order bride. A replacement bride."

"That may be how it started, but I can tell it's more than that now. Jesse stayed home with you after your accident and cared for you himself. I would call that a smitten man. I certainly wouldn't do it for Phyllis."

"She's your wife."

"Ah, but there's the rub. I only married her to get the mine. You see, she was Phyllis Hopper before she became Phyllis Nelson."

"What did you do to the rest of her family?"

"They went to California. At least, that's what she thinks. Actually, her parents are buried out back of this cabin. You see, I found the vein on their claim. The only way I could get my hands on it was to marry Phyllis, so I did and then I sent Ma and Pa to heaven."

"Oh, my God. You're a murderer. Phyllis probably thinks you love her. The way she looks at you, she's certainly in love with you. And you...you killed her parents."

"I know. That's why manipulating her was so easy."

"You're despicable. What will you do with me?"

He shook his head and lifted his brows. "It's so sad. Jesse is going to murder you, and I, having come upon the scene, will kill Jesse, but not before he has disposed of you."

"You think you have it all worked out, but you don't. Jesse will save me, and you won't kill him."

"An optimist to the last."

"Boss, something's wrong. Jesse is riding up but he's got the sheriff and three of his deputies with him."

"What?! That can't be. How could they be here already? He can't have had that much money on hand."

Suddenly Will pulled his pistol out of its holster and pointed it at Harry.

"No, Boss, no."

Will fired.

Harry fell.

Clare screamed and dived for cover under the table.

Jesse slammed open the door to the cabin.

"Drop the gun, Will."

Will dropped the gun. "It was self-defense, Jesse. I…he—"

"Jesse!"

Clare ran to him

He caught her with his free arm, but never lowered his pistol or his gaze from Will Nelson.

"Are you all right?" Jesse asked her.

Sam Longworth was right behind Jesse, along with his deputies.

"We've got this. You take Clare home."

Jesse holstered his Colt, then stopped and looked at Clare.

"You ran straight to me. You said you're sight is back in the note. For how long?"

She nodded. "Since Harry brought me here. That's why I can tell you Will shot Harry in cold blood. Not self-defense. He and Phyllis are the ones behind the accidents. He murdered Phyllis' parents, too. They're buried behind this cabin."

Jesse tightened his hold on her with his left arm and brought his right hand up, setting two fingers against her lips.

"Shh. Everything is fine now."

He leaned down and kissed her fully, then wrapped her tighter in his arms.

"When I found Nora and the note you wrote, I was thrilled and scared for you at the same time."

"You were scared?" She tried to keep the hope from her voice.

"Afraid I might not be in time. Sam had one of his deputies following Will for some time. He wondered about Mr. and Mrs. Hopper when they disappeared so suddenly after Phyllis married Will. That was only a year ago. It has taken this long to finally catch him."

"Nora?"

"She'll be all right. She's got a goose egg on her head and will have to take it easy for the next few days. Then she'll be right as rain."

"I'm glad. Thank you for coming for me."

"Of course, I came for you. You're my wife."

"And," she prodded.

"And what?"

"And you care about me. As a matter of fact I think it's more. I think you love me."

He set her away from him.

"I don't think so. After what Rebecca Jane did, I'll never love another woman."

"I'm not Rebecca Jane. I'm here. I'm your wife."

"That doesn't matter. You could change your mind and leave."

"I could, but only if you chase me away."

"Why would I chase you away?"

"I'm asking myself the same question." Clare looked at the door. "Let's just go home and leave this ugliness behind. Sam can take care of them."

"I planned on taking you home. Nora is beside herself with worry. Tell me about your vision."

She tried to forget that he said he couldn't love her. She knew he must. If he didn't love her why was he so kind and caring when she lost her sight. Nora could have taken care of her.

"I was amazed. When it started coming back, I wasn't sure that is what was happening. Everything was gray rather than black, but I still couldn't see shapes or movement. Then when Harry shoved me down on the bed, it must have jarred something and I could make him out, in color, I was ecstatic. He was blurry but I could see his brown hair. I wanted to shout to the rafters, but had to maintain that I was blind so that he wouldn't blindfold me."

He took her back into his arms.

"Have I told you how brave you were?"

"No."

"No? That's very negligent of me. You're the bravest woman I've ever met and I'm honored to call you my wife."

He lowered his head and gave her a kiss. A real kiss. The kind she'd been missing since her accident. One that heated all her insides and sent them roaring to her core.

Surely he felt the pull just like she did. That kiss couldn't have had no effect on him. Could it?

*****

Clare continued to take things easy. The doctor wanted her to wait a full week after her vision returned before she resumed her normal routine. She had to admit he was probably right. Her vision improved more each day until she could finally see everything clearly.

She sat up in bed, shortly after Jesse got up. "I can see you gave up shaving. Why?"

"I thought, since you couldn't see me anyway, I'd let the beard grow."

"I can still feel you when you kiss me. I understand why you stopped kissing me, but I miss your kisses."

He came back to the bed.

"You miss them, huh?"

"Yes. I do."

Jesse dropped his drawers got back under the covers.

"Did you miss just my kisses?"

Butterflies fluttered in her stomach. "No, I…"

"You…what?"

"I missed you. I missed your making love to me." She reached over and ran her fingers down his jaw. His beard was soft. "Make love to me, Jesse."

His fingers lightly touched her from her stomach around her breasts over her nipples and up to her chin, where he cupped her jaw. "I thought you'd never ask."

His lips claimed hers, and the only thing that mattered in her world was him. Jesse. This moment. She felt as though she'd only lived for this.

*****

All the feelings Jesse had for Clare scared him. He knew he'd be hurt if he gave in and loved her. Rebecca Jane showed him what happens when you love a woman. They don't keep their word. They take your heart and tear it in two.

A small voice told him that Clare wasn't Rebecca Jane, but Jesse didn't listen. He went back to the mine and drowned his sorrows in work.

When he got home around midnight, he was surprised to find Clare curled up and asleep in the leather chair in his office. He looked down at her sweet face and couldn't imagine life if she left him. But she would.

He wouldn't get too close. He'd protect his heart this time…wouldn't let Clare hurt him the way Rebecca Jane had.

He picked her up out of the chair and carried her to bed. Maybe he'd try avoiding her tomorrow. Tonight he was holding his wife and imagining what life would be like if she loved him and planned on staying.

*****

Clare checked the calendar again she hadn't had her menses for two months. There was no doubt in her mind…she was expecting. Would Jesse be happy? Of course he would, but was the prospect of a baby enough to make him love her?

Why hadn't she noticed before? Well, she'd had a lot happening…the accident and losing her sight, getting kidnapped. Wearing only her chemise and bloomers, she walked over to the long mirror hanging on the wall and looked at herself. She touched her stomach, and then turned sideways. Could she tell? Maybe there was a small bump or maybe she was seeing what she wanted to see.

She turned away and finished dressing before going downstairs for breakfast.

Nora sat at the kitchen table with a cup

coffee.

"Are you ready to eat?"

"Oh yes, I'm famished."

"I've got pancakes, with sausage, bacon and all the coffee you can drink."

"That sounds wonderful."

Nora started to stand.

Clare put a hand on her shoulder.

"I can serve myself. Since I can see again, I don't need to be waited on any longer."

"As you like."

Clare dished up a plate full of the succulent offerings.

"I feel like I haven't eaten in days."

She sat at her place at the table and began eating with vigor. Suddenly, her stomach turned upside down. Her eyes widened. She ran to the sink and lost all of the breakfast she'd just eaten.

"Well, I guess that proves it," Nora said as she handed Clare a towel.

"Proves what?" Clare wiped the sick away from her lips before rinsing her mouth with a glass of water.

"That you're in the family way."

"How would you know that? I just realized it myself."

"I do the laundry, and you haven't used any rags for your menses since I have been here."

"All right. I think I am, but I'm not telling Jesse yet. Not until I'm sure. I'll go see Dr. Kilarney today. I need to have him check my eyes anyway."

"I won't say anything. Not my place."

Clare sighed and leaned back on the sink. "What am I to do, Nora? Jesse says he'll never love me because of what Rebecca Jane did. If he can't love me, how am I to raise this child in that kind of situation?"

Nora shook her finger at Clare. "Listen to me, girl. Jesse does love you. He stayed with you and cared for you when he could have left you to me. But, he wouldn't have any of that. He loves you. Think about all the little things he does that make you smile. The naughty things he whispers in your ear that make you blush. When he brings you a bunch of wildflowers even when you couldn't see them because he knows you'll like them. How he never gave up on you regaining your sight."

Clare nodded. "That all makes it sound like he loves me, but I don't know. I just don't know."

"What don't you know?"

Jesse walked into the kitchen from outside.

Clare jumped and then stood away from the sink.

"I…ah…don't know why I'm feeling sick. I can't keep my food down."

She could be honest with him that far.

"You should go see the doctor. Maybe you've caught an illness."

"Yes, I think I'll do that." Clare set the towel on the counter and pumped water into the sink to rinse it out. "In fact, I'll go right now."

"Fine. Good," said Jesse.

"I'll see you later."

"Are you walking or riding?"

She held on to the back of her chair at the table. "Walking. It's a pleasant day. Not too hot yet and I thought I'd stop and see Jo. Maybe play with the baby for a bit."

"All right. I'm going to the mine. I don't know when I'll be home, I've a lot of work to do. Don't wait up for me."

Clare nodded, afraid her voice would betray her disappointment.

Jesse had spent more and more time at

the mine and less with her. She guessed she'd gotten spoiled having him home during her recovery.

She left a few minutes after Jesse did, walked quickly to Jo's and knocked on the door.

"Clare." Jo held a sleeping baby. "I'm just putting Paul down for his morning nap."

"I hope you don't mind me stopping by unannounced."

"Not at all. Come on in, we'll have time for a visit while he sleeps."

Clare closed the door behind her and sat on the sofa while Jo took Paul to his bedroom.

When Jo returned, she sat on the couch across from Clare.

"I'm pregnant," Clare blurted out.

"Well, I'm not surprised." Jo grinned. "It was bound to happen eventually."

"But Jesse says he doesn't love me. How can I raise a baby in a house without love?"

"You know, I thought that about Sam. He told me he'd never love a woman again because they would die."

"Well," Brows wrinkled, Clare cocked her head. "Of course we die. Everyone dies."

"I know that, but he was afraid to be hurt again, so he determined to never fall in love. But, as he admits now, he never loved his first wife. He felt guilt over her dying after she left him." Jo leaned back against the sofa and closed her eyes. "You know I could just sleep now."

"I'm sorry, you probably should be napping while Paul does."

"Nonsense. If I wasn't talking to you I'd be doing housework and I'd rather visit with you. Clare, believe me. Jesse loves you."

Clare sat forward and clasped her hands in her lap. "So you think Jesse will come around and realize he loves me?"

"Probably, but not without some prodding. It might take drastic measures on your part but if I'm correct he will definitely realize that what he feels is real love."

A ray of hope burst forth in her chest. "I'm ready to try anything. Just tell me what to do."

CHAPTER 14

Jo closed her eyes.

"I had to leave Sam before he realized that he loved me. You don't want to do that I don't think, do you?"

Clare shook her head. "I don't. Going home, knowing I'd given up on my marriage, my parents would be so disappointed in me."

"Have you always worried about what your parents thought of you?" Jo reached over and placed her hand on Clare's knee. "Have you always tried to please them? You can't you know. Parents always want what is best for their children and when we don't achieve that which they were expecting, they're disappointed. We may be the happiest we've ever been, but that doesn't change that we aren't what they thought we should be."

"I was never good enough for my parents. They wanted me to be a boy. I'm the oldest you see and Pa didn't get his son for awhile. There were another three girls before my youngest sibling, Adam, was born. Pa built up a lot of resentment and I felt it. As a girl I wasn't pretty enough to get a husband. I was too fat, too tall, too strong, or whatever. I just wasn't right."

"I want you to forget all of that. You will never go home as less than triumphant. You've married a rich man who loves you, whether he realizes it or not."

Clare nodded. "I have, haven't I? Getting Jesse to realize how important I am to him is the problem. I already know how important he is to me."

"And I know how important you are to him. I want you to seduce your husband. Get a new nightgown. One that doesn't invoke nightmares."

"Nightmares?" Her nightdress wasn't that bad...was it?

"You have to admit your nightgown is

horrible."

"It doesn't matter, Jesse would have it off of me in no time. He hates them. Since I quit wearing one, I never thought to replace the one I had."

"Well, maybe he just hates that one. I know I do. At least make what he's taking off attractive. After Paul wakes up, let's go up to the mercantile and see what Lavernia has in her special section in her back room, just for women. She stores her prettiest nightgowns, lingerie and dresses, back there."

"She does? I never knew."

"She doesn't share that information with everyone."

"Tell you what. I have to see Dr. Kilarney, have him check my eyes and confirm my pregnancy. After that I'll come back here and we can go see Lavernia."

"That sounds good. Paul should be awake by that time. Lavernia loves being with him, so does Effie at the hotel. He's got two wonderful grandmas in those two. I can see my son being very spoiled."

Clare smiled and stood. "I'd best be going. See you soon."

Jo walked her to the door. "Don't worry

about Jesse. He'll come around."

"I hope you're right."

Clare walked up the street past the hotel, the butcher, and the mercantile. She traveled to the end of the boardwalk and continued on past the Nugget Saloon and the Branch Water Saloon to Dr. Kilarney's home and clinic. The one-story white house with green shutters sat back from the street.

She knocked on the door and then entered.

"Doc? It's Clare Donovan. Are you here?"

"I'm coming." The doctor walked out to his waiting room and took Clare's hand. "How are you doing? Did you walk all the way here?"

Clare nodded. "Yes, I did."

"Did you have any discomfort? Did the sunlight hurt your eyes?"

"No. No discomfort and the light did not bother me."

"Good. Very good. I think you can go back to your regular routine."

"That's wonderful news. I think I have some other news that I want you to confirm for me."

The doctor lifted a brow. "All right.

What is it?"

Clare wrung her hands. "I think I'm expecting a child."

He smiled. "Well, that's great news. Come with me back to my examination room, and I'll check you out."

Thirty minutes later, Clare walked past the mercantile on her way to Jo's with a smile on her face. Doc had confirmed she was pregnant and, based on her record of her cycle, he guessed about two months. That would mean she probably got pregnant with the first few times she and Jesse made love.

She reached Jo's house and knocked.

Jo opened the door.

"Come in. What did Doc say?"

"He said yes." She was absolutely giddy with the news. "About two months."

"My that's fast." Jo gave her a big hug. "You've only been married about three months now, isn't it?"

"In another week we'll have been married three months. I've decided that I'm telling Jesse at bedtime tonight. I want to look at Lavernia's collection for ladies. I'd like to be dressed in something pretty when I tell him."

"Paul's awake. I just changed him. Let

me get him dressed and we'll go see Lavernia."

When they walked into Smith's Mercantile, they were the only customers in the store.

"Lavernia," called Jo. "I have a customer for the back room."

"Why, Jo, Clare, how are you both today?"

"We're both wonderful," said Jo.

"Yes, wonderful," repeated Clare. "How are you today?"

"I'm just dandy. Thank you for asking," said Lavernia. "Now, I understand that you want to take a gander at my back room. Is that right, Clare?"

"Yes, ma'am. I need a new nightgown."

"Ah, I see. I take it you don't want one of the flannel ones out front?"

"No, ma'am. I want something that Jesse will enjoy seeing me in."

"I have just the thing. Come with me."

Lavernia took Clare's hand and tugged her behind the counter to the back room.

In the storage room behind the rest of the store, Lavernia had two large cedar wardrobes. She walked to the one on the left side of the room and opened it. Lavernia waved her arm in front of the hanging clothing. "This is where I have my special things with lace from Brussels and silk from Paris. Just because we live in the remote country, is no reason we can't have lovely things, too."

"Oh, my gosh." Clare couldn't believe her eyes. She'd never seen so much silk and lace in her life. Her gaze roamed over the collection, and a pale peach gown caught her eye. "That one." She pointed at the nightgown.

Lavernia pulled the frothy confection from the closet.

"I wondered if that one wouldn't catch your eye. With your red hair and pale skin, it should look lovely."

Clare held the gown up to her and checked it for size. It looked like it would fit her curves nicely.

"I'll take it. Put it on Jesse's bill."

"Yes, ma'am," said Lavernia. "Do you want the robe that goes with it?"

"Oh, yes. The entire set. I don't even want to know how much it costs, because if I know, I'll think twice about getting it."

"She'll take it all," said Jo quickly.

"I'll wrap it up for you."

Lavernia took the two pieces of clothing off the hangers and walked out to the front counter.

Clare and Jo followed.

"Don't forget," said Lavernia. "If you need anything else, I have these wardrobes back here and I can order whatever you need if I don't have it."

*****

For the walk home, Clare clasped her package to her chest. She couldn't wait to try them on and see how they looked. She would leave her hair loose and not braid it tonight. Jesse liked it down. He liked to let her hair pour over his fingers, said it 'feels like silk'.

Now she really did have some silk he could run his hands over. Would he like it? She hoped so and was willing to take that risk for the chance of saving her marriage.

*****

Jesse worked until he thought Clare would already be in bed. He'd been doing his best to avoid her and it was darn difficult. She seemed determined to be with him. He'd go home and find her asleep in a chair in the parlor or at the kitchen table, or on the sofa. Each time, he'd shake his head and carry her upstairs to bed.

In bed, he stayed on his side so as not to pull her into his arms, but that didn't matter. In her slumber she scooted over until she reached him, then she'd throw an arm over his stomach and relax back into sleep.

How was he supposed to combat that?

He couldn't. Every morning he awoke with their arms and legs entangled. His fault as much as hers. He craved her touch, whether he wanted to or not. They hadn't made love in two weeks, and he was about to go insane, his lust for her boundless. But he was determined he would not touch her, he would keep her safe. There would be no children. Nothing to keep her here, but if he forced her away what was he proving? Not that women leave, just that they leave him, because he pushes them away. Would it have been different with Rebecca Jane if he'd loved her and brought her with him from the beginning?

Tonight, he didn't find Clare downstairs anywhere. That was good. She'd actually gone to bed, which surprised him. Maybe she was giving up and would leave. Even though that was the outcome he desired, he was disturbed at the thought.

He found a plate of leftovers on the warming shelf above the stovetop. Jesse grabbed a fork and knife before sitting at the table to eat the beef stew and bread with gusto, as though he was starving and it was his last meal. After he was done, he put his dishes in the sink and headed for the stairs.

When he reached the bedroom, the door was closed. They never closed the door unless they were making love, and so the entrance had been open for a while now.

He opened the door and crossed into the room. The lamp on the bedside table burned low, casting a soft, warm glow. Clare was asleep on top of the covers. She'd been waiting for him and wore a beautiful nightgown. He'd never seen her in anything but that ugly old thing and this was definitely not that.

Jesse shed his clothes and lay down next to Clare.

She woke, sat up, and shoved her beautiful mass of hair away from her face.

"Jesse?"

"Yes, it's me."

"I waited for you. I wanted you to see me. I bought a new nightgown just for you. Want to look at it?"

Clare didn't wait for his answer but crawled to the side of the bed and then stood. She wiped the sleep from her eyes, looked back over her shoulder at him and smiled. Sashaying as she walked around the end of the bed, she used her hands to swirl the fabric of the skirt back and forth so he caught a glimpse of her leg as she moved.

Mesmerized, his mouth dropped open.

Clare chuckled, walked to the bed, bent over, giving him a eyeful of her lush bosom, and used two fingers to raise his chin and close his mouth.

"I take it by your response that you like it."

Jesse tried. He really did, but how could he resist this siren he'd married. She was trying so hard and all he did was reject her. But he couldn't tonight. He reached up clasped her around the waist and brought her body flush with his and then turned her until she was under him. He lowered his head and took her lips with his and drank his fill of her special wine.

He gathered the peach frock in his hand and pushed it up her legs.

"Raise for me."

She responded to his guttural command

and lifted her body so he could shove the gown above her waist.

He positioned himself and buried all he had to give in her willing body. This he could give her. Love, he couldn't.

*****

Jesse loved her all night long. She'd expected him to be next to her when she finally woke up, but the bed was cold. He was gone. She wanted to cry and she hadn't told him about the baby, maybe that was for the best if he couldn't stand to be near its mother. What kind of parents could they be?

Clare put on the robe that matched the nightgown and went downstairs to the kitchen.

"Wow!" said Nora. "That's some dressing gown you have there. You look wonderful."

"For all the good it did me." Clares shoulders slumped. "Jesse made love to me all night and couldn't be bothered to say goodbye this morning. I thought we were making headway. I was wrong."

"Now, honey. Jesse's just scared. Give him time to come to terms with what he's feeling."

"I've been giving him time. I wait up for

him, or at least I try to. He's been coming in really late, and I, well, in my condition, I can't seem to stay awake. He always carries me to bed, but he's gone in the morning. I thought today might be different since we made love, but it isn't. Nora, I don't think he'll ever love me."

Nora took a deep breath. "I don't know if he will or not. He's a pretty stubborn man. Rebecca Jane hurt him terribly, keeping him on the hook like she did. I don't know that he'll ever change his mind about women after something like that."

"And I can't live in a home without love. Not with the little one on the way."

"What will you do?"

"I don't know. I'm going to talk to Jo. I may go to my parents, though I don't want to."

"Then don't. Fight for your marriage. Fight for the love you know he feels but won't recognize."

"How do I do that? I tried seducing him and it worked so far as we had sex, but that's not love."

"That was one time. Don't give up. Go to Jo's. Stay there for the time being. You're close enough that you'll begin to show soon and he'll see that."

"I don't want him to take me back just because of the baby. I'd rather raise the child by myself in a home full of love rather than live with Jesse and his denial."

CHAPTER 15

Clare packed her bags. Nora would take care of Jasper, she'd promised the kitten wouldn't go hungry. Clare walked down the street to Jo and Sam's house. She knocked on the door.

Jo answered.

"Come in." She stood back and held the door for Clare to enter. "It didn't work I take it."

"Oh, I seduced him all right," angry tears burned her eyes. "But he left before daybreak and who knows when he'll be back. Can I stay with you for a while?"

"Of course, you can."

"Will Sam mind? I don't want to cause

trouble."

"It's no trouble," said Sam as he walked in from the bedrooms with Paul in his arms. "I was coming to see you anyway. Will Nelson's trial is coming up in a couple of weeks. You'll have to testify."

Clare nodded. "I knew I would. I just didn't know when. What will happen to Phyllis? Did she know Will killed her family?"

"He says she did know," said Sam. "She says she didn't. The judge will have to decide who is telling the truth. But, I have nothing to hold her on, so she's free until the trial. Then she'll come in and testify against her husband. Here, let me take those bags to the bedroom. Trade you."

He handed Paul to Clare and took away her bags.

"I hope you don't mind sharing with Paul. He sleeps through the night now." Jo stopped and smiled. "Or at least he doesn't make any noise to get us up."

Clare grinned at the baby and was rewarded with a toothless grin back.

"We'll be just fine. I love the idea of sharing the bedroom with the baby. Come on, Paul, you can help me unpack."

"This will be wonderful. I'll have a built-in babysitter, so I can get caught up on my housework."

"You should call on me when I'm home, I'll still watch the baby. I love him. I love babies. I can't wait to have one of my own."

"Give it a few months after she's born."

"She?" Clare lifted her eyebrows. "You think I'll have a girl?"

Jo pick a piece of clothing from the basket she'd set at her feet. She folded the garment and put it on the coffee table in front of the sofa where they sat. "Don't really know, but I hate calling the baby an 'it'. She's a person. Sam always wanted a boy, so I thought of our baby as a boy until he was born, then he was Paul."

"I hope I have a girl." Clare said softly. "But, I'll be happy with a boy, too. I guess what I really want is for the baby to be healthy, boy or girl." She lifted little Paul to his feet and held him lightly while he stood on her lap. "Jo, look how strong he is."

Jo looked up and smiled. "He loves to stand. I think it's because he can see more. He can see your face, not just your chest."

Paul giggled.

"Oh," laughed Clare. "I guess you do

like standing up."

Sam came back out of the bedroom.

"I'm leaving you ladies and heading to work. I have a feeling today and tomorrow will be bumpy days."

"Why?"

"When Jesse finds out you left, he'll be here demanding you come home," said Sam.

"No, he won't." Clare's eyes filled with tears that she refused to shed. "He'll be glad to be rid of me. He's been working late and trying, most successfully, to avoid me, ever since I got my vision back. I thought he'd be happy I wouldn't be incapacitated but he's been mean ever since."

"What do you mean when you say he's been mean?" Sam's eyes narrowed. "I don't care that Jesse's my friend. If he's been physically—"

"No!" Clare shook her head. "He hasn't hit me. It's just that he works all the time so he can avoid me. He comes home after I've fallen to sleep, usually in the chair in the parlor or at the kitchen table, trying to wait up for him. And he leaves before I wake up. Until last night, I couldn't tell you if Jesse had a beard or not, because I hadn't seen him in two weeks. Believe me he'll be happy I'm gone."

"I thought that with Sam, too," said Jo, glancing at Sam. "But he wasn't. He was just—"

"Afraid. I admit it," said Sam.

He hooked his thumbs in his pockets as though he needed to put his hands somewhere.

"I was afraid to be with her, but even more afraid to be without her. Jesse will come around."

"I think you're wrong, but I hope you're right."

Three days later, Clare knew Sam was wrong.

Jesse didn't come around to collect her. He didn't even send Nora to make sure she was all right.

Nora came on her own. She, Jo, and Clare sat at Jo's kitchen table, each with a cup of coffee.

Nora set her coffee on the table and wrapped her hands around the warm cup.

"I had to know that you are still here and holding up. Jesse has been a bear to live with."

"At least he's coming home at a decent hour and you get to see him," said Clare bitterly. She took a sip of her coffee. "Jo, are there any of those cookies I made left, or did I eat them all?"

"No, you didn't. I managed to save a few from you and Sam. Goodness gracious." She looked at Nora. "The way they go through sweets you'd think they were both pregnant, not just Clare."

"I'd rather Jesse go back to not being seen," grumbled Nora. "The way he is, I'm not sure how long I can take living there myself."

"I'm so sorry, Nora. This is my fault. Perhaps I should move back home."

"No!" said Jo and Nora together.

"You have to stand up to him and make him come to you," said Jo.

Nora waved a hand. "Don't mind me. I'm staying with the crazy man unless he fires me."

Clare's eyes filled with tears. Who would have thought I'd have such wonderful friends?

"Oh, don't cry, honey." Nora came around the table and wrapped Clare in her arms. "Everything will work out fine. You'll see."

"I think I'll go home to Golden. Maybe

having me so close is all he needs. He can see me when he wants, and obviously he doesn't want to talk to me. So I'll make it hard for him to."

"I don't think that's the problem," said Nora. "He's grumpy because he misses you, and he doesn't know why. He doesn't believe he could love you, and by you leaving and going to Golden, he'll believe he was right. Women leave. By staying here with Sam and Jo, hopefully he'll realize that—"

"That he was right." Clare sat straight and flicked a glance between the women. "I left. I should have stayed and fought. I'm going back home, but I'll sleep in the guest room. Maybe he'll get the hint. Will you help me pack? I'm going home now."

Jo raised her eyebrows and looked at Nora. "Are you sure? With Sam, I didn't move back until he came for me."

"But Jesse isn't Sam." Clare stood and started for the guestroom. "Jesse believes he isn't lovable because Rebecca Jane didn't love him. Well, I do love him and I mean to make sure he understands that I'm not leaving no matter how ornery he gets."

Twenty minutes later Clare hugged Jo

goodbye.

"Thank you for letting me stay, and for helping me to understand my husband. I wouldn't have without coming here." She turned to Nora. "Are you ready?"

Nora nodded. "Yes, let's get you moved back in and be waiting for him at supper when he comes home."

"The worst that can happen is he goes back to working all the time. But, I'm telling him about the baby and that I'm staying unless he bodily throws me out, and even then I'll be back."

They walked back to the house, and Clare put all of her things away in the guest bedroom. She wouldn't allow them to have marital relations, but she would live in her home. No one was chasing her away. Not anymore.

*****

A knock sounded from the front door.

"I'll get it, Nora," called Clare from the parlor where she was reading. She set her book aside and walked to the door.

"Phyllis." Clare was taken aback. She lifted her eyebrows and slightly cocked her head. "What are you doing here?"

Phyllis Nelson, a tall, willowy blonde,

stood on the front porch.

"I came to see you and Jesse, of course. Aren't you going to invite me in?"

Clare backed up. "Certainly. Come in."

She walked past Clare and into the parlor.

"I always loved this house. I told Will we needed to build a new house because since Jesse built this one, ours was only second best. And I deserve the best. Do you know why?"

Clare shook her head. "No, I don't."

"I am the one who came here with my parents when there was no one here but miners and a couple of prostitutes. I'm the one who dug and sifted for gold alongside my parents. I'm the only woman in this town who knows what it is to suffer and go without. I married Will because it was expedient to do so. He said he was on his way to California and I could get away from Hope's Crossing and into some place more civilized."

"I don't think I understand what that has to do with me, but why don't you sit and I'll have Nora get us some tea."

Clare started to walk to the kitchen.

"No," Phyllis pulled a small derringer

from her purse. "Don't be fooled by its size. This gun can kill you. I should know. I saw Will use it on my parents, at my request. Don't you see, there wasn't enough for all of us. Only Will and me."

"Now, Phyllis." I have to figure a way out of this. I have to protect my baby. "Even if you kill me you still have Jesse to deal with."

"But you see, that's just it, I'll kill you both. Call your woman." She jutted her chin over her shoulder toward the back of the house.

"Why?" Clare feared that Nora would be the first to die if she called her in.

"I want her to go get Jesse."

"I won't let you kill him," said Clare.

"Don't tell me you've fallen in love with your husband."

Phyllis laughed.

Cackled was more like it. The sound was one made by someone who was a bit unhinged.

"What if I have?"

Phyllis stood stock still, pointing the gun at Clare. "He'll never love you back. Jesse isn't capable of loving anyone. I should know. I tried to get him to marry me before

Will came along. But he had that fiancée in New York. He was sure she would come out here, and when she didn't, he shut down. Then he decided to send for you. He wanted someone to warm his bed, that was all. He'll never love you."

"You're wrong, Phyllis. I just couldn't love you."

Jesse's rich baritone came from the hallway to the kitchen. He entered the parlor with his Colt in hand.

"Put down the gun, Phyllis and we all live."

Phyllis whirled at the sound of Jesse's voice, her gun now pointing at him. "No. This is not the way it was supposed to happen. I've been watching, waiting for her to come back. I knew she would, she's in love with you, you see."

"I'm glad to hear it. I discovered when she left that I love her, too. I was just too stubborn to admit it."

Clare gasped and tears filled her eyes. Her heart fluttered and she could hardly believe her ears. Jesse loved her. That was all that mattered.

Sam came through the front door, and now both he and Jesse held their weapons aimed at Phyllis Nelson.

"Give up, Phyllis. There are only two ways this ends; with you in custody, or with you dead. Which is it to be?"

Phyllis looked from Jesse to Sam and back again. With a sob, she lowered her derringer and fell to her knees, a broken woman.

Jesse ran to Clare, whose legs threatened to quit supporting her, and took her in his arms.

"I'm sorry. I never meant to hurt you. I was scared." He held her tight to him, like he would never let her go.

Clare clung to him, her arms clasped around his waist. "Jesse, I'm sorry, too. I should never have left. I won't ever again, whether you tell me you love me or not. I will never leave you."

"You won't have to." He gazed down at her, his beautiful blue eyes glistened. "I love you Clare Donovan with all my heart."

"Oh, Jesse. I love you, too."

Jesse took Clare's hungry lips with his own and kissed her deeply, completely.

She'd missed those kisses. Missed his touch.

"I've got her now, Jesse. You and Clare

can finally relax," said Sam.

Clare and Jesse broke apart and both looked toward Sam. He had Phyllis' hands behind her back in handcuffs.

"You and Will can occupy the cells next to each other now." Sam led Phyllis out of the house.

"How did you know to come?" asked Clare as she gazed into Jesse's eyes.

"Nora. She heard what was happening and came to get me. Rode Buttercup bareback up to the mine. She actually caught me coming home, and when she told me what was happening, I galloped all the way here. I had her take the horses to the barn and told her to stay there. I should go get her now and let her know it's all over."

Jesse hugged Clare tight.

"I'm so glad I wasn't too late."

"So am I. When you come back, meet me upstairs. I have something for you."

Jesse cocked his eyebrow, but nodded.

"I'll be right back."

Clare climbed the stairs to her and Jesse's bedroom. There would be no guest room for her, now or ever.

She paced the floor, waiting until she heard Jesse's boots as he ran up the stairs.

The sound stopped just outside the bedroom door. She pictured him taking a deep breath before coming in, and smiled.

Jesse entered and closed the door behind him.

Clare had the curtains open, and the light from the window illuminated the room.

"Clare, again, I'm sorry."

She rushed to him and put her fingers lightly over his lips.

He wrapped his arms around her waist and held her loosely.

"There is nothing to be sorry for. I shouldn't have expected you to love me so soon. Just because I fell in love with you, doesn't mean you did me. I know that now. I was the one who was wrong."

"No. You were right. I was afraid to admit my feelings for you."

"I'm not Rebecca. I love you, Jesse Donovan."

His arms tightened.

"Don't ever stop."

"I won't. I promise."

His lips crashed down on hers, and he delved inside.

She loved the taste of him. Nothing was as good.

She pulled back and looked up at him.

"I have some news I hope you'll like."

"What is it?"

"I'm expecting. We're having a baby."

Jesse's eyes widened and he smiled as he hugged her tight.

"That's wonderful." He let her go and sat on the bed. "I'm going to be a father. Me. A father."

Clare sat beside him.

"Yes. You. Are you happy about it?"

"I...I...yes."

He took her face gently between his hands.

"I'm so happy I don't know what to say. I can't believe I'll be a father. When? How soon?"

"About seven months."

"Seven months, and we'll be parents."

Suddenly, his smile faded.

"Are you all right? What about making love? Will I hurt you?"

She laughed, delighted that he wanted to make love and that he worried about her. "No, I think we'll be fine."

"Good. Because I want you naked, Mrs. Donovan. I've missed you."

Clare stood and began opening the

buttons on her dress.

"Not as much as I've missed you."

Soon they were both naked, and Jesse had Clare in his arms as they lay on the bed. He kissed her gently, slowly sipped her lips, then he moved to her neck and she turned her head to give him better access.

He started to move lower.

Clare stopped him.

"I need to know that what happened today is behind us. Make love to me, Jesse. Make love to me, now."

"Your wish is my command."

EPILOGUE

Seven or so months later

Jesse paced back and forth in front of the fireplace in the parlor.

"How can this take so long?"

Sam sat in one of the Queen Anne arm chairs and read a book.

"Just because it didn't take long to make the baby doesn't mean it's not taking long to be born. Babies come in their own sweet time. I learned that with Paul. So, what names have you picked out?"

Jesse sat in the chair opposite Sam.

"We chose Sean if it's a boy and Colleen if it's a girl."

"Are they after your parents?"

"No. We decided that we could do better than our parents, but with a name like

Donovan, we should go after my Irish roots. They are names that Clare liked. I let her pick the names since I really don't care. As long as the child is healthy, I'm happy."

"That's nice. I'm sure she appreciated the gesture."

"Nope. Said I was making her do all the work now."

Jesse couldn't sit. He jumped up and began pacing again.

"Did I tell you how glad I am that you're here? I'd be breaking down that door if you weren't here telling me it's normal for those sounds to come out of my wife."

"I had my father, Paul, with me when I went through it the first time."

Jesse stopped pacing and looked at Sam. "First time?"

"We didn't want to say anything yet. This is your and Clare's big day."

"Nothing's going to change that. Are you and Jo expecting again?"

Sam grinned.

"Yeah, due in five or six months."

"Well, congratulations."

"Are you letting Jo name this one, or will you name it together like you did Paul?"

"Probably together. We're hoping for a

girl this time."

Jesse nodded. "We'll probably use the name that doesn't get picked this time for the next one, if it's that gender."

"I don't care about anything except the baby and Jo. As long as they are all right, she can call the baby the devil himself."

A small cry sounded from upstairs.

"The baby. He's here."

Jesse ran up the stairs two at a time and burst through the open doorway.

"Clare. Are you all right?"

"Jesse."

She sounded tired. Her voice weak.

He ran to the bed. His beautiful wife was sweaty and bedraggled like she'd been working in the mines for hours upon hours.

"Clare, sweetheart, how are you?"

"I'm tired, but so happy. Look."

She opened the swaddling on the small bundle next to her displaying a child with bright copper hair and blue eyes.

"Her hair is like mine was when I was small. It will change. Her eyes, I don't know. They say all babies have blue eyes, so hers could stay blue or change to green like mine." She stroked the baby's cheek. "We won't know until she gets older. Are you terribly disappointed she's not a boy?"

Jesse remembered Clare telling him how disappointed her father had been with her because she was a girl, not a boy.

"No, my love. I love her just as she is. Did you decide to name her Colleen?"

Clare shook her head.

"I changed my mind. When I saw her, I thought Laura. Her name will be Laura Colleen Donovan."

"I like that. Laura."

He reached down and took the baby's hand with his finger. She was so small, but she wrapped her hand around his finger, and he swore he felt her squeeze it. After that, he was hers. She had him wrapped around her little finger, and he would do anything to protect her and see that she had the best life he, as her father, could provide.

Dr. Kilarney washed his hands in the basin of clean water. The other basin had been removed by Jo and given to Nora to dispose of.

"You did real well, Clare," said the doctor as he wiped his hands dry walking back to the bed. "Little Laura is eighteen inches long and, according to my scale weighs six-and-one-half pounds. All within the bounds of normal."

Clare smiled up at the doctor. "Thank you, Dr. Kilarney. I'm so glad you were here to deliver her."

"Ah, you didn't have anything to worry about. You had Jo and Nora both here to help. You'd have been fine."

"I know," said Clare. "But I'm still glad you were here."

"Me, too."

Jesse shook the doctor's hand and then gave him a twenty-dollar double eagle gold piece.

"I don't charge that much for delivering babies, Jesse. Just five dollars."

"I know, Doc, but you delivered my special girl and kept Clare safe. That's worth a lot more than the twenty dollars I gave you. Whatever you need, you let me know, and I'll see you get it. All right, Doc?"

Doc Kilarney laughed. "All right, Jesse."

"Do I get to see the little sweetheart?" Sam stood in the doorway.

"Of course. Come in." Jesse picked up Laura and held her for Sam to see.

"Isn't she beautiful?" He gazed down at his daughter.

"That she is. Maybe she and Paul will

marry, one day. The only for sure thing is that they'll play together as they grow up." Sam reached over and ran a finger down the baby's cheek. "She's so soft. Babies always have the softest skin."

"That they do." Jo came up behind Sam and peeked over his shoulder. "It's time for us to take our leave and let this family get better acquainted."

"You're right." Sam bent down and kissed Clare on the forehead. "You did very well, Clare. Very well, indeed."

"Thank you, Sam. And Jo, thank you for being here to help the doctor and Nora."

"You're welcome. Of course, you have to do the same for me in about six months." Jo flashed a grin and cupped a hand on her belly.

"Oh, how wonderful. You're expecting again. Why didn't you say anything?"

"Because, this time is for you. My time will be coming up."

Clare waved her over.

"Bend down and let me kiss you."

Jo bent down and showed Clare her cheek.

Clare kissed her. "Thank you."

"It was nothing you wouldn't do for me.

Let's go, Sam, before Paul gets tired of watching his grandson."

"That will never happen." Sam looked over at Jesse and Clare, then chuckled. "Those two are thick as thieves."

Jesse followed as the doctor and the Longworths left. He closed the bedroom door behind them and walked back to the bed. Sitting, he kicked off his boots and lay down next to Clare with little Laura between them.

"Thank you for my daughter."

He leaned over and kissed Clare full on the lips. Not a subtle little kiss but one full of passion.

"I will always love you, Jesse Donovan. You are my heart. Without you I can't survive. And Laura is our joy. The proof of our love for each other."

Jesse heart overflowed with love, knowing he could finally believe those words. He reached over and cupped Clare's face.

"I love you, too, Clare Donovan. Forever."

He looked down at Laura.

Her eyes were open and she sucked her fist, seemingly as happy as her parents.

She was the first, but not the last child born to Jesse and Clare Donovan of Hope's Crossing, Montana.

ABOUT THE AUTHOR

Cynthia Woolf is the award winning and best-selling author of twenty-two historical western romance books and two short stories with more books on the way.

Writing as CA Woolf she has six scifi, space opera romance titles.

Cynthia loves writing and reading romance. Her first western romance Tame A Wild Heart, was inspired by the story her mother told her of meeting Cynthia's father on a ranch in Creede, Colorado. Although Tame A Wild Heart takes place in Creede that is the only similarity between the stories. Her father was a cowboy not a bounty hunter and her mother was a nursemaid (called a nanny now) not the ranch owner.

Cynthia credits her wonderfully supportive husband Jim and her great critique partners for saving her sanity and allowing her to explore her creativity.

TITLES AVAILABLE

THE REPLACEMENT BRIDE – Hope's Crossing, Book 2

THE HUNTER BRIDE – Hope's Crossing, Book 1

THORPE'S MAIL-ORDER BRIDE – Montana Sky Series – Kindle Worlds

GENEVIEVE, Bride of Nevada, - American Mail-Order Brides Series

GIDEON – The Surprise Brides

MAIL ORDER OUTLAW – The Brides of Tombstone, Book 1

MAIL ORDER DOCTOR – The Brides of Tombstone, Book 2

MAIL ORDER BARON – The Brides of Tombstone, Book 3

NELLIE – The Brides of San Francisco 1

ANNIE – The Brides of San Francisco 2

CORA – The Brides of San Francisco 3

JAKE (Book 1, Destiny in Deadwood series)

LIAM (Book 2, Destiny in Deadwood series)

ZACH (Book 3, Destiny in Deadwood series)

CAPITAL BRIDE (Book 1, Matchmaker & Co. series)

HEIRESS BRIDE (Book 2, Matchmaker & Co. series)

FIERY BRIDE (Book 3, Matchmaker & Co. series)

TAME A WILD HEART (Book 1, Tame series)

TAME A WILD WIND (Book 2, Tame series)

TAME A WILD BRIDE (Book 3, Tame series)

TAME A SUMMER HEART (short story, Tame series)

TAME A HONEYMOON HEART (novella, Tame series)

WEBSITE – www.cynthiawoolf.com

NEWSLETTER - http://bit.ly/1qBWhFQ